Patricia Wallace

MONDAY'S CHILD

ZEBRA BOOKS
KENSINGTON PUBLISHING CORP.

ZEBRA BOOKS

are published by

Kensington Publishing Corp.
475 Park Avenue South
New York, NY 10016

First printing: September, 1989

Printed in the United States of America

For Andy
and
For Michael Andrew
who was born on a Sunday

Monday's child is fair of face . . .

Prologue

January, 1982

Dr. Noah Huston stood near the clinic window looking out at the night. The rain beat relentlessly against the glass, driven by gusts of wind that rattled the heavy panes. It had been storming for hours now and showed no sign of letting up.

Diagonal sheets of rain blew across the deserted industrial park and were colored momentarily by the red glow of the traffic lights which blinked a warning to the empty streets. Below the light standards, rainwater churned and foamed at the storm drains which, as usual in Southern California, were unable to handle the flow. The intersection was rapidly flooding.

Somewhere distant, a siren wailed, but it was no match for the wind, and the sound was borne away.

Either that or the chill coming off the window made him shiver.

"Dr. Huston," a voice said from behind him, "are you sure you don't want anything?"

He shook his head, then turned. "You're really going out in this?"

Margot Reed gave him a rueful smile. "Got to eat, you

9

know. Besides, what's a little rain?"

"*That* is a monsoon."

The nurse laughed. "I'll risk it. There's an order of onion rings out there calling my name."

"Ah, well, onion rings. As long as you've got a good reason."

"The best. Armies aren't the only ones who travel on their stomachs."

Huston watched as she shrugged into a child-sized yellow slicker, then tied a plastic raincap over her dark hair. Twenty years his senior, the tiny woman at five feet nothing weighing perhaps ninety pounds, looked as though a good stiff breeze might carry her off.

"Maybe I should be the one to go," he said.

"Thanks for the offer, but I'm dispensable. You're not; the sign outside says 'Physician on Duty.'"

"But—"

"There's no 'but' about it," she said in the no-nonsense way nurses had. "This is a Doc-in-the-Box. If you leave, it's a Box, period. Then we're out of business, and I'm out a paycheck."

"No one's exactly knocking down the doors—" Sunday nights could be deadly quiet, even without a storm to keep the patients away.

"Nevertheless." She started purposefully down the hall towards the rear entrance. "I'll be back before you know I'm gone."

The icy air that rushed in when the door opened raised the hair on the back of his neck and sent him to the doctor's lounge searching for a mug of hot coffee to wrap his fingers around.

When he returned to the reception area, he thought at first that Margot had changed her mind, and that the rain had driven her back, but then he realized that the woman

10

standing in the shadows was enormously pregnant. Judging by the look on her face and the way her right hand wandered restlessly over her belly, she was in labor.

Her cotton maternity dress was drenched, and it clung to her thickened body. Dripping strands of dark blond hair were plastered to her head.

Huston looked past her, toward the parking lot, expecting to see whoever had brought her here, or at the very least the car in which she'd driven herself, but the lot was vacant. Had she walked?

"How did you—"

"Please," she said, her voice oddly breathless. "The baby is coming now."

She leaned heavily against him as he guided her toward an examining room.

Get her settled, he thought, and call for an ambulance to transport her to the nearest hospital; the clinic served the light industrial factories which surrounded it, handling mostly worker's comp cases, but wasn't equipped to deliver babies.

More to the point, he hadn't attended a birth in over a year, since he'd completed his residency.

"Oh," the woman gasped, her body tensing with pain. She stopped short of the doorway and gripped his wrist with cold fingers. "Now. It is now."

"Now?"

A look at her face convinced him.

Somehow he maneuvered her the rest of the way into the room and managed to lift her up onto the padded table. There wasn't time for modesty; he pulled the wet dress up above her hips and grabbed a pair of bandage scissors to cut off her underwear which he noted was stained with bright red blood—the perineal tissue had begun to tear.

11

He quickly determined that she was late in the second stage of labor, and fully effaced. The baby was crowning, the top of its head visible.

"*Merde,*" she whispered.

"I'll second that," Huston said. He turned from the table, his eyes scanning the glass-enclosed shelves for a surgical pack that might contain instruments he could improvise with. He wanted to perform an episiotomy before the perineum tore further.

Behind him, the woman had begun to pant.

"Hold on," he said. He grabbed a suture kit, a disposable scalpel, a pair of Latex gloves, and a package of sterile surgical towels, placing everything on the procedure table. He ripped open the outer wrapping of the suture kit, opened the packet containing the scalpel, then slipped his hands into the gloves.

It had taken only seconds, but when he approached the woman again, he saw that it was too late for matters of finesse; the birth was imminent.

He placed his hand over the baby's head. The brow was presenting, then he applied a gentle pressure, allowing the head to advance.

As sometimes happened, the face was covered with a membrane, the caul, but even as he reached to clear it away, it changed color, turning a bluish-black.

"What the hell?"

The caul dissolved, giving off a coppery odor.

Huston blinked, drawing back involuntarily. Granted, he was no obstetrician, but he'd never seen that happen before, had never heard of such a thing. He glanced at the woman, but her eyes were blank and unseeing, her face contorted by the pain.

He took a deep breath, and returned to the task at hand. He carefully rotated the baby, positioning it to deliver the anterior shoulder, then lifted the head slightly, which allowed the posterior shoulder to slip free. With an ease that never failed to amaze him, the baby was expelled. He caught the tiny body, glistening wet and slippery from the vernix caseosa.

It was a girl, he saw, and perfectly formed.

Huston turned the baby, since he had no bulb syringe to aspirate the nose and mouth, and held her up by her heels to let the fluid drain. He took a surgical towel and used a corner of it to wipe out the infant's mouth.

A tremor ran through the small limbs, and the baby finally took her first breath.

The exhalation was black.

He very nearly dropped her. Whatever had come from her lungs hung in the air for a heartbeat, and then dissipated before his startled eyes.

Unable for the moment to think, he stood transfixed, watching the baby "pink" in his hands. His professional instincts took over then, and he placed the infant on her mother's abdomen. He tied off the umbilical cord in two places, a couple of inches apart, using lengths of sterile gauze as ligatures.

As he reached for the scissors from the suture kit, he noticed that the baby had opened its eyes and appeared to be looking at him.

For some reason, that unnerved him, and he hesitated, his hand poised over the surgical pack.

Thunder sounded nearby, close enough to shake the building. Overhead, the fluorescent lights dimmed, fading to near dark before coming up again.

With the threat of a power failure as impetus, he took the scissors and cut the umbilical cord.

Belatedly, he glanced at the clock; it was seven minutes after midnight. Monday morning, then.

* * *

Huston wrapped the baby girl in a blanket he'd taken from the warmer, and carried her to the exam table in the room directly across the hall. He surrounded her with sand bags, which were usually used to immobilize patients with neck injures, to keep her from harm.

He still had to deliver the placenta, but there was no hurry for that, and he went to the phone on the wall to call for an ambulance. He dialed 911 and listened through static as the line rang.

Turning, he could see partway into the first room, see the lower third of the exam table, spatters of blood on the floor beneath it, but he couldn't see the mother.

He frowned. Was she sitting up?

The line continued to ring, unanswered.

Huston moved towards the door, stretching the phone cord to its limit, trying to get a better view, but it looked, from where he stood, as though no one was in there. Had the woman gotten up? Was she foolish enough to try and leave before delivering the afterbirth?"

"Shit," he said, dropping the phone, thinking of blood loss, a sudden catastrophic hemorrhage.

He ran the five steps to the opposite doorway where he stopped, or *was* stopped, by a wall of air so cold that it numbed his face.

His mind struggled to make sense of what his eyes beheld, but there was no sense to make of it; in his experience, it could not be happening.

The woman stood beside the exam table. Her skin was abnormally pale, almost cyanotic. But he realised in that same instant that she was beyond pale; she was, he saw, transparent.

He could see *through* her.

A moment later she quite simply disappeared.

*   *   *

"What in the world?" Margot's voice preceeded her down the hall.

Huston looked in her direction, feeling dazed. He hadn't heard her come in.

"It's freezing in here." She peered at the thermometer on the wall and rapped it with her knuckles. "I think it's colder inside than out."

"Margot," he said, and fell silent, painfully aware that anything he might say would sound absurd. If he had been in practice twenty years, maybe someone would believe him, but as the new kid on the block—

"Stupid thermostat . . . and you need one of those Allen wrenches to adjust the darned thing." The nurse put a white take-out bag on the counter.

The smell of fried food made his head swim. Or maybe, he thought, it was a delayed reaction. Whichever, he leaned against the doorframe for support.

"What's this?" Margot moved past him into the second room. The phone still twirled on its cord, emitting a disconnect signal. She retrieved it and hung it up. When she turned, she was facing the table where the baby lay. Her eyes widened and then she glanced at him.

"Look at what the wind blew in," he said.

Huston told them—first the ambulance attendants and then the police officer who arrived a few minutes later—that he had gone to the lounge for a cup of coffee and when he came back, he discovered that someone had left the child just inside the clinic door.

He hadn't seen anything, hadn't heard anything. Caught off-guard, as anyone would be, given the circumstances, he unfortunately hadn't had the presence of mind to watch for a car driving away.

He produced a slightly stained white towel which he

15

claimed the baby had been wrapped in when he found her. In fact, he'd gotten the towel from the clinic lost-and-found box while waiting for the ambulance to arrive. He'd considered writing a note—"Please take care of my baby"—but decided against it.

Keep it simple, he told himself. Don't complicate matters.

As it was, there was no reason to doubt his story; these things happened. Babies were abandoned, and not always in ways that contributed to their survival.

The cop stifled a yawn, looking bored, as he took notes for his report.

When the paperwork was done, the baby was transported by ambulance to Children's Hospital.

After they were gone, Margot went into the examining room and cleaned up the blood without comment, working with her usual brisk efficiency. She put the instruments in solution before autoclaving them, then bundled up the soiled linens and threw them into the laundry cart.

She discarded the ruined underwear along with the Latex gloves, shoving them to the bottom of a bag of trash.

"Thank you," he said when she'd finished.

"Any time." Curiosity showed in her eyes, but she asked no questions.

Which was good, he thought, because he had no answers to give.

Later—much later—he heard from a social worker that the child had been placed with a local family for adoption, but that after a week, the family had returned her to the Agency for reasons they'd preferred not to state.

A second placement had a similar outcome, this time

within twenty-four hours.

Finally, just before the baby's first birthday, she was taken in by a third couple who, to the relief of everyone, adopted her.

The family name was Baker.

The child they named Jill.

Thursday

One

Georgia Baker held the jar at eye level and carefully moved the edge of the knife along the inside surface, trying to get every last bit of peanut butter. She ran the tip under the rim and then scraped repeatedly at the bottom of the jar, making a face at the annoying sound of blade on glass.

Tiny peaks of peanut butter remained here and there; from experience she knew that these were impervious to knife or spoon, and that it was an exercise in futility to even try.

Some bright person, she thought, could make a fortune by inventing a device to get those elusive dabs.

"Or," she säid under her breath, "a not-so-bright person could have gone and bought another jar." She tossed the empty into the trash.

She reached for a slice of wheat bread and spread what she had managed to salvage on it. The peanut butter covered all four corners of the bread, although not by much. She'd have to remember to buy smaller bread from now on.

Jill was fussy about what she ate, and she liked her

peanut butter at least a quarter of an inch thick, but today this would have to do.

Which reminded her—

"Jill," she called, raising her voice to carry down the long hallway. "Honey . . . you're going to be late. The bus will be here any minute now."

From somewhere in the general direction of her daughter's bedroom a door squeaked shut, apparently in response.

No "I'm coming, Mom."

No "Just a minute."

For the last six months or so, Georgia had felt as if she might have become The Invisible Mom. Was she now inaudible as well?

She sighed and covered the second slice of bread with strawberry jam—there was plenty of that—and slapped the two together. She cut the sandwich diagonally, then eased it into a Baggie. After licking the jam from her fingers, she grabbed for a twist-tie.

"Morning."

She glanced up. Dave came in buttoning the cuffs of his shirt. That done, he crossed the kitchen, opened the refrigerator door and stared inside.

"You left the 'good' off," she said, turning the twist-tie the requisite three times.

"Hmm?"

"The good." At his blank look, she continued: "You know, as in 'Good morning?'"

He frowned and half-shook his head. "We're out of orange juice again. And eggs."

Georgia didn't comment. She'd scrambled the last egg for Jill, who hadn't wanted it. Maybe he wouldn't notice if she dug it out of the garbage? Ten seconds in the microwave and it would be as good as new.

"Not even an English muffin, I see."

"No. Sorry." She selected the least-bruised apple from

22

the fruit bowl, held it under the faucet in what was probably an ineffectual attempt to rid it of pesticides, and dried it with a clean corner of the dishtowel.

"You'd think that once in awhile, there'd be something to eat around here," Dave said, and let the refrigerator door swing closed. "I mean, food essentially represents our very livelihood—"

Not yet it doesn't, she thought, and immediately felt a twinge of guilt. Every business went through rough times to start with, and the restaurant wouldn't always be in the red. Would it?

"—and you certainly never see butchers without meat on the table, or tailors going without clothes."

Georgia smiled faintly. "Or candlestick makers going without candles."

He gave her a sour look. "It's a little early in the morning for whimsy, don't you think?"

She didn't, actually.

"Is there coffee at least?"

"Yes." She inclined her head in the direction of the coffeepot as she wrapped the apple in a paper napkin to cushion it and put it in Jill's lunchbox. "But there's no cream—"

"You *are* going to make it to the store today, aren't you?"

"I guess I'd better." Add one more thing to the list of things to do after work.

He gave a nod of satisfaction. "Oh, and this is the last clean shirt I have."

"Damn."

"What?"

"Nothing." The dryer was kaput again, and the repairman couldn't fit her in before next Wednesday. Nor could he be bribed—or at least, not at a price she could afford—so she'd had to hang the wash on the sagging clothesline in the back yard.

23

Naturally, she'd forgotten to bring them in. With all the foggy nights they'd been having, no doubt everything was as wet now as they had been when she'd taken them out of the washing machine.

"And Georgia?"

She heard the subtle change in the tone of his voice and looked up, her hand pausing in mid-air as she reached for the cookie jar.

"If you happen to talk to Cosgrove today, I want this inheritance thing resolved."

"Dave—"

"No, I mean it. I know she's your little sister and you want to be fair to her, but she hasn't got a leg to stand on. The old man's will was very specific—"

"—and very unfair."

"That's debatable, but even so, this situation has dragged on long enough. And I shouldn't have to remind you that we can't collect a cent until everything's settled. You know we need the money."

"So does Bev . . . she's raising Katy on her own."

"That was her decision."

Georgia heard the disapproval in his voice and for a second it was as though the years had slipped away and it was her father speaking:

"You're eighteen years old, Beverly Jean, and the law says you're an adult now, so it's your decision to make, but if you insist on having this baby, you're no daughter of mine."

Of course, her father should have known that telling Beverly not to do something was the single best way of making sure she did it.

"Anyway," Georgia said, shaking off the memory, "Mr. Cosgrove is out of town until Monday."

"That figures. Lawyers." Dave frowned into his mug, made a face, then crossed to the sink and poured the coffee, almost a full cup, down the drain. "Well, I've got to get going. I'll probably be late again tonight, so don't hold dinner for me."

She started to come around the counter to give him a good-bye kiss, but he'd already turned on his heel and was gone.

A moment later she heard the front door slam, followed in short order by the sound of the Blazer's engine starting up and then by the squeal of tires as Dave backed out of the driveway.

Georgia reached the window in time to see the tail lights flash as he slowed for the four-way stop sign on the corner.

"And you have a nice day, too," she said.

Two

"Jill?"

Her mother's voice came from outside her bedroom, and Jill turned quickly at the sound, hiding her hands behind her back, and curling her fingers around the smooth round shapes.

There were two raps at the door before it opened. Her mother stood framed in the doorway, the hint of a frown on her face.

"Jill, didn't you hear me call you?"

She shook her head.

"Well, you've missed the bus again. That's two times this week."

"I'm sorry." It was what she was expected to say, whether or not it was true.

"And why aren't you wearing your new dress?"

"Dress?"

"Honestly, Jill . . ."

Her mother came into the room then, crossing directly to the closet. The dress was off to one side, still in the clear plastic garment bag in which it had come from the seamstress. Her mother unzipped the garment bag and slipped the dress off its hanger.

It was peach-colored, made of something called dotted

27

swiss, with puffy little cap sleeves and a full skirt over three layers of petticoats.

The petticoats rustled, annoying her with their whispers.

She hated the dress, hated everything about it, except, of course, for the—

"Today's the day they're taking your school pictures, isn't it?"

Jill felt a catch in her throat. She watched as her mother fussed with the white velvet sash and had to repress a shudder. "Yes," she said, waiting for her mother to notice what she'd done.

"Then you should wear this." Her mother held the dress up to the window to catch the light, and Jill saw the familiar soft look in her eyes. "You'll be the prettiest girl in your class."

"But . . . I'll be late."

"*Now* you worry about being late. It'll only take a minute for you to change. I have to drive you to school anyway; I can take a shortcut."

Jill took a step backwards, her legs pressing against the bed. "The buttons came off."

"What?"

"The buttons." She held her hand out; in her palm rested the six pearl buttons which had decorated the front bodice. "They came off."

"Oh, Jill."

It was more a sigh than anything else.

"What is it with you and buttons? They didn't just fall off, did they?"

"Some of them did."

"Hmm. However it happened, there isn't time to sew them on now."

Jill said nothing. There was no mistaking the disappointment in her mother's expression. She watched with mild curiosity—and relief—as her mother walked to

28

the closet and hung up the dress.

"Come on, then, off to the car with you. And leave the buttons on the nightstand so I'll know where to find them when I get a minute. At least you can wear the dress to Easter services."

No!

She hadn't spoken, but the word resounded through her head.

Her mother had already turned away.

On impulse, Jill closed her fist around the buttons. A thrill of heat surged through her fingers. When she opened her hand a moment later, what she saw made her smile.

She dropped the small misshapen lump onto the polished surface of the nightstand and followed her mother out of the room.

Three

Cheryl Appleton stood at the front of the classroom, surveying the frenzied activities of her second graders and wondering if it would be possible to find out what genius had invented the artificial "grass" used in Easter baskets.

More importantly, she wondered whether a jury of her peers would convict her for shoving about a ton of it up the inventor's nose.

There was hardly a square inch of the room not covered with the stuff, in both green and pink. Crinkly strands of it were visible in most of the kids' hair, and she saw a thick wad slowly drift down to the bottom of the aquarium where no doubt it would prove fatal to the few remaining fish.

Even the air was full of it, in the form of spitballs of both hues.

No question about it, she thought. The only possible verdict would be one of justifiable homicide. Arguably she might be seen as performing a service to mankind.

Enough was enough.

"Class!" She called as loudly as she could, but was drowned out by the din of excited young voices. She tried again. "Class! Children!"

31

At the back of the room, Mrs. Bastilla, a parent volunteer, seemed to be the only one who heard, and she held a finger to her lips to hush the children.

The children ignored both of them.

Miss Appleton opened the top desk drawer, pulled out an old-fashioned copper cowbell, and rang it vigorously, but to no avail.

A howitzer would have had a hard time being heard over the racket these kids were making.

Two of the girls looked vaguely in her direction, as if they thought maybe they should, but nineteen other precious darlings continued what they were doing, which now included stapling pink and white paper bunny ears to articles of clothing, and, quite possibly, judging from the decibel level, the skin beneath.

Some of the boys had taken to squashing the yellow marshmallow chicks and were making dying chicken sounds, which precipitated a flood of tears from the more sensitive of the girls.

Kevin—her choice as poster boy for retroactive birth control—had lined up a row of candy hummingbird eggs and was shooting them at his classmates. The projectives missed their targets as often as not, and hit the windows like pastel-colored hail.

The school day was twenty minutes old.

Worse than that, it was only Thursday. Tomorrow, the day before Spring Vacation began, would be twice as bad, what with the Easter pageant and all. All those kids, strung out on sugar and chocolate, and rabid at the prospect of a week off from school . . .

Fun and games.

Miss Appleton sighed and sat at the desk, reaching for her attendance book to take the roll.

At least she could pretend to be in charge.

*　　　*　　　*

She had just marked Jill Baker absent when the door opened and Jill came in.

By chance, at precisely that moment, there was a marked quieting of the room, and Miss Appleton rose quickly to take advantage of it.

"All right," she said with as much authority as she could muster on short notice. "I want you all to go back to your desks and sit *quietly* until Mrs. Bastilla and I set up the activity tables."

Surprisingly, there were no arguments.

With an orderliness that the nuns from her own school days would have approved of, the children returned to their seats, except for Jill who approached her with a note from the office.

Miss Appleton took the note and tucked it between the pages of the attendance book to read later. "Thank you, Jill. Go and sit down, please."

"Yes, Miss Appleton."

She waited until Jill had taken her place and all eyes were facing front. She wasn't sure how she'd regained control of the classroom, but since she had, she intended to make the most of it.

"While we're setting things up *again*, I want you to take out your folders and work on your Easter cards."

"Mine's finished," a voice piped up from the back of the room.

Kevin, of course. "Oh? Then you can—"

"I wrote a poem. You want me to read it?"

"That won't be necessary." The boy did have a knack for poetry, but some of the words he liked to rhyme weren't fit for reading out loud.

"Miss Appleton?"

"Yes, Jill?"

"I finished mine, too," the child said, her dark eyes serious.

Unaccountably, the hair at the nape of her neck began

33

to prickle and she rubbed at it absently. "That's fine. You and Kevin can have fifteen minutes of free time—"she gave Kevin a significant look—"make that *quiet* free time on the Apple."

Kevin gave her a look back—that of a condemned man resigned to his fate—then got up and walked slowly to the computer corner where he was joined by Jill. He stood aside, for once the perfect little gentleman, as Jill booted up the computer.

The other children had already turned their attention to their Easter projects. The only sounds in the room were those of paper rustling and the clacking of the computer keyboard.

Hard to believe this was the same classroom or these the same children. Except that a number of them were sprouting bunny ears . . .

If she knew what she'd done to restore calm, she'd write it up for *California Teaching*.

Or maybe *Amazing Stories*.

With the children settled for the time being, Miss Appleton headed to the activity tables where Mrs. Bastilla was attempting to resurrect some of the less mangled marshmallow chicks.

"I think they're done for," she said gently.

"Done for," Mrs. Bastilla, who didn't speak much English, agreed.

Four

Kevin Browne was careful to stand back, well out of the way. As an extra precaution, he shoved his hands into the pockets of his jeans and then tucked his elbows in close to his body. He breathed as quietly as he could, which, because he had a cold, was through his mouth.

Jill Baker appeared to be unaware of his presence as she worked intently at the computer, but he knew differently. He knew better.

She was never unaware.

Spooky, how nothing seemed to get past her.

Some of the other kids thought she had eyes in the back of her head. Since his last name came after hers in the alphabet, he'd had plenty of opportunities to check out the back of her head, and so far he hadn't come across a second pair of eyes.

That didn't mean they weren't there.

An avid fan of scary books and movies, Kevin believed *anything* was possible. Lately, he had come to suspect that she was an alien lifeform from another planet in a far away galaxy.

Aliens were particularly good at disguising their alienage, although there was usually something that gave them away. A fondness for reptile breakfasts or green

35

blood or dissolving in the rain . . . .

Alien or not, the very last thing he wanted to do was get her mad at him.

Again, a little voice in his head whispered. *Don't get her mad at you again.*

Kevin had been living dangerously lately. Sometimes he couldn't help it.

"You're asking for it, Kevin," his mother always said, and maybe she was right.

On Monday, he'd tried to glue Jill's books together, squirting practically a full container of Elmer's Glue-All between her Reader and her math workbook, but the stuff didn't have a chance to dry and all he'd wound up making was a mess.

He was good at messes.

At morning recess on Tuesday he'd accidentally on purpose kicked a soccer ball directly at her while she was playing hopscotch, waiting until her back was to him, but she'd jumped aside at the last moment and then gave him a look that had made his insides churn.

And yesterday, when everyone was lining up to go to the auditorium for the Easter pageant rehearsal, he shuffled his feet across the carpet and then reached out to touch Jill, giving her a jolt of static electricity.

Jill looked as though she might like to give *him* a charge. Something dark and dangerous was going on behind her eyes.

But Miss Appleton had come along the line just then, telling everyone to face the front, stop talking, and act like young ladies and gentlemen.

Saved!

There wouldn't always be someone coming along to save him, he knew, and he also knew when he was treading on thin ice. As the youngest in a family of five boys, he'd developed a fine sense of when he'd reached that point beyond which retribution waited.

Knowing when to stop was the only thing that had kept his brothers from killing him, and it was what kept his hands in his pockets now.

Jill Baker frightened him.

The thing was, a part of him *liked* being scared. He liked the feeling he got when the hair on his arms stood up or when his heart raced and icewater seemed to flow through his veins.

He enjoyed the sensations of fear.

Even just standing this close to her made his muscles tingle, and he had a kind of fluttering in his stomach. Neither were unpleasant feelings.

Once he'd tried to tell some of the other guys how he felt and they'd misunderstood.

"Kevin loves Jill, Kevin loves Jill," they taunted.

A couple of the girls in his class had overheard and they joined in the torment, probably because Jill was absent that day and they felt safe. Before long, all the kids on the playground were singing:

"Kevin and Jill, sitting in a tree, k-i-s-s-i-n-g. First comes love, then comes marriage, then comes sister in a baby carriage."

It was one of the few times in his life that he'd been glad when recess was over.

He didn't love her, or any girl.

In fact, of all the girls he didn't love, he didn't love Jill more than any of them.

His mother and father called Jill a heartbreaker, and his brothers teased him about her, because they said she was pretty and when she grew up, watch out.

Kevin would die before he'd admit it, but he knew they were right, except he thought she was pretty in the way that certain spiders were. Being pretty didn't make them any less deadly.

As for the part about being a heartbreaker, *that* he could believe.

He oftened wondered, if he made her mad enough, would she pull his heart out of his chest and break it before his dying eyes?

A shiver ran up his spine.

"Kevin," a voice said from behind him.

Startled, he jumped and, off-balance with his hands still in his pockets, fell against the wall. He struck his left shoulder and elbow hard, bringing sudden tears to his eyes.

Jill turned from the computer, her hands resting in her lap.

Miss Appleton looked at him and shook her head. "Honestly, Kevin. Sometimes I think you're an accident just waiting to happen. Are you hurt?"

"No."

"Sure?" At his nod, she continued: "The two of you can come join the others now. We need to get the Easter baskets finished."

Jill had gotten up, and he stayed back, leaning against the wall, as she passed by him. She came close enough that he could smell the lemony scent of her hair and, in spite of his resolve not to, he found himself looking at her.

She gave him only the briefest of glances, but it felt very much as though her fingers were closing around his heart.

Without a thought as to the consequences, he stuck out his tongue.

Five

"Georgia?"

Georgia looked up from the list of new acquisitions to see Faye Paxton standing in the doorway, a curious smile on her face.

"I'm sorry, Faye," she said, taking off her reading glasses, "were you talking to me?"

"I think maybe *at* you. It's past one. You want to go have lunch?"

"Lunch?"

"You know, what most people eat between breakfast and dinner." Faye came into the small cluttered office and began to sort through a box of books that one of the patrons had donated to the library. "Or have you chained yourself to the desk again?"

"No, I can take a break," she said after glancing at her watch. Where had the morning gone? She penciled an X on the invoice to mark her place and then stood up. "But I do need to run a couple of errands, if you don't mind."

"You know me, I never mind," Faye said, closing the book she was holding and returning it to the box. "More errands, huh? I guess he's really got you running in circles, doesn't he?"

It struck her as an odd remark, even coming from Faye, and Georgia looked at her with a frown. "What on earth are you talking about?"

"Nothing. Not a thing."

"Faye . . ."

"Just making idle conversation."

"You? When have you ever?"

"I am now."

Georgia regarded her skeptically. It wasn't like Faye to be evasive, or for that matter, tactful. She'd never been one to shy from asking the most intimate of questions, nor did she hesitate to offer advice, unsolicited or otherwise.

Reticence was simply not in Faye's makeup.

"You know you can't keep a secret no matter how hard you try," Georgia said. "You might as well tell me now and save yourself the aggravation."

"Since you put it that way . . . I guess someone has to, and I'd rather you hear it from me. But—" Faye took her by the arm and led her towards the door "—I think I'd better wait until we're somewhere more private."

"Where's more private than here?"

"Are you kidding? The ventilation ducts in this place act like amplifiers. A careless word and it'd be all over town in a minute, if it isn't already."

"*What* would be all over town?"

Faye's expression was grim. "You don't have a clue, do you?"

At Faye's insistence, they went to eat first. Settled in a booth at Hamburger Haven, Georgia waited until they'd ordered their lunches and the waitress had brought

40

their drinks.

"Well?"

Faye busied herself with her iced tea—squeezing the lemon wedge, adding two packets of sugar, and stirring. And stirring.

"What are you doing?" she asked finally.

Faye avoided meeting her eyes. "This isn't easy."

"Just tell me."

"I will. Only let me do it my way." She folded the empty sugar packets into neat squares. After a moment she took a deep breath and looked up. "I went out to dinner last night."

"Yes?"

"To Baker's."

"And?"

"Did you know that Dave hired a new hostess?"

Georgia sat back. "He told me he was going to. I know he was interviewing, trying to find someone to take Linda May's place while she's having her baby. I didn't know he had."

"Then you haven't met her?"

"No, obviously I haven't."

Faye ran a manicured thumbnail along the crease of her napkin. "She's gorgeous."

"Is she?" Georgia attempted a smile. "That ought to bring in the business."

"Funny business, maybe."

"No, really. An attractive hostess is an asset to any restaurant."

"Well, honey, she was certainly swinging her assets around."

"Faye . . ."

The waitress chose that moment to arrive with their food, giving them each other's order and spilling the au jus for Georgia's French Dip in the process.

41

"Enjoy," she said with a snap of her gum, and quickly disappeared.

They switched plates.

"Anyway," Faye said, probing her Chef's salad with her fork, "they seemed to be very friendly."

"As opposed to being unfriendly? I don't see the harm in that."

"I mean *friendly*."

Georgie felt the heat rise in her face. "I assume they remained clothed?"

Faye's eyes widened. "Whoa! Don't get mad at me. I'm only telling you what I saw."

"No, you're telling me your interpretation of what you saw. What really happened?"

"Well," Faye put down her fork and leaned forward, lowering her voice, "they were kind of whispering and laughing when we first got there, and then later she was standing at the reservation counter and he came up behind her and put his arm around her."

"That's it?"

"It all seemed a bit too cozy, if you ask me."

"Listen, I appreciate your concern, but I think you're making something out of nothing." She dipped a french fry into the au jus, twirled it, but didn't eat it. "I've seen him do the same thing with Linda May."

"Linda May is happily married, perpetually pregnant, and not, if I may say so, a raving beauty. This girl is trouble with a capital T."

"Trouble," Georgia said, smiling faintly. "Right here in River City?"

"I wouldn't make light of it, if I were you."

Georgia reached across the table and patted her friend's hand. "Don't worry so much. Dave and I are fine."

"Are you?"

"Yes."

Faye held her gaze for a moment before nodding slowly. "All right. Good." She picked up her fork and speared strips of turkey and cheese. "God, I'm famished, aren't you?"

"Starving," Georgia said. But she didn't eat.

There was an auxillary post office in the same small shopping center that housed Hamburger Haven, and Georgia went in to mail the bills—better late than never—and buy stamps. Not wanting to stand in line, she fed five dollars worth of quarters into the vending machine, made her selection and turned to leave without waiting for the book of stamps to drop.

Faye followed after her and tucked the stamps into the outside compartment of her purse. "You forgot these."

"Did I? I don't know where my mind's at."

Faye only smiled and shook her head.

At the pharmacy door she picked up a refill of Dave's sinus medication and nearly walked out without paying for it.

"So," Faye said, hurrying to catch up with her, "how is Jill these days?"

"Jill's okay," Georgia said. "Except for having a button fetish."

"Buttons?"

"She collects them." Georgia paused, shading her eyes to look in a display window.

"Hmm. Kids are strange."

"I don't know, I used to collect all kinds of weird things when I was her age. Which reminds me, I wanted to get her an Easter present."

"In here?" Faye peered in the window. "This is an

43

auto parts store."

"No, no. I've decided that she's old enough now to have a pet."

"What, a goldfish or something?"

"I was thinking of a bunny."

Pet Corner had a corral full of bunnies and it took some doing, but Georgia found the perfect one, a black and white flop-eared dwarf rabbit.

The rabbit's fur was unbelievably soft and she stroked it gently, marveling at the feel of it. She could feel the animal's heart racing and she cuddled the small form to her, trying to soothe the poor thing before putting it into a separate holding pen.

She then selected a cage, feeding bowls, rabbit chow, vitamins and other necessities, arranging to have everything delivered to the house after work. As the cashier was ringing it all up she added a book: "How to Care for Your New Rabbit, Or You're No Bunny till Some Bunny Loves You."

The total came to seventy-six dollars and thirty-nine cents.

"Ouch," she said, looking at what was left of her cash. "Will you take a check?"

"Sure, with I.D. and a major credit card."

She dug out her checkbook but upon opening it, she groaned.

Faye peeked over her shoulder. "As bad as that? Need a loan?"

"It isn't that; I've got the money," Georgia said, although that wasn't exactly true. She tore out the top check. "I forgot to give this to Jill for her school pictures. She was late this morning—"

"Ma'am?" the clerk interrupted. "Seventy-six thirty-nine, please."

"Oh, sorry." She scribbled hurriedly. "Faye, don't let me forget to call the school. I want the pictures, and I don't think they'll even take them unless you pay in advance."

Faye laughed. "Don't be silly. As pretty as Jill is, there's not a photographer in the world who could resist that face."

Six

The photographer peered through the viewfinder of the Pentax, squinting at his hundredth or so small face of the day and pulling it into focus.

"Okay, now smile," he said, resting his finger lightly on the shutter.

The boy, a freckled, homely little kid with a butch haircut, grinned fiercely into the camera. Two of his front teeth were missing and he had a scab across the bridge of his nose. Apparently the boy had been picking at the scab which was peeling at the edges, exposing the raw-looking skin underneath.

"Good. Now, you know what to say?"

"Cheese!" the boy responded with enthusiasm. The tip of his tongue was clearly visible between the gap in his teeth.

It would take a singularly devoted mother to love that face, the photographer mused as he snapped the shot. "Perfect."

"Don't dawdle, Jeffrey," Miss Appleton, the second grade teacher said, whisking the boy out of the chair. "Others are waiting."

"There's no hurry," the photographer said. He straightened up slowly, feeling the strain of hours spent bending over in the tight aching muscles of his lower back. "I have to change film anyway."

But the teacher had already ushered in the next child, and gone off to hunt another.

The photographer smiled at the little girl. It wasn't hard to do; she was a stunner. Her chestnut brown hair framed a delicate heart-shaped face, and her eyes were a remarkable gray-green, a shade he'd never encountered before in a lifetime of noticing such things.

She was slight of build, but even at her tender age there was already a femininity about her, a gracefulness of line and form, that caught the eye and held it with the promise of the years to come.

Promise, yes. Definitely.

He refused to allow himself to speculate on how she would look ten years hence.

Unlike the other girls, who'd worn their frilly pastel Easter dresses, this exquisite child wore a plain gray jumper over a black silk blouse. Tiny gold earrings were her only adornment.

Not that she needed more; she was a beautiful, beautiful child.

"I'll be—" he had to stop to clear his throat "—I'll just be a minute."

A hint of amusement played at the corners of her mouth. She sat down on the chair, smoothed the skirt of her jumper, crossed her legs primly at the ankles, and then looked up to meet his eyes.

Unaccountably, he found himself fumbling with the camera, as though he'd never changed a roll of film before. The rewind crank resisted his attempts to grip it, and he swore under his breath.

Miss Appleton had returned, another youngster in tow, and she gave him a curious look as he struggled to do what normally he could have done in his sleep. The arch

48

of her eyebrows reproached him which didn't help matters.

What was it about second grade teachers, anyway? Forty-odd years since he'd been a second grader, and he still got a sinking feeling in the pit of his stomach at that if-you'd-listened-in-class-you'd-know-the-answer expression they all wore.

He had, he realized, begun to sweat.

"Will it be," Miss Appleton said, "much longer?"

"It will be as long as it takes," he answered through clenched teeth.

"We have a schedule to keep."

"So do I." He popped the back of the camera and removed the film canister. "And if you don't mind, I work better without an audience."

"Well!" Miss Appleton huffed. "There's no need to be rude." She turned abruptly and walked away, the child she'd brought following in her wake.

Through all of it, those gray-green eyes were watching him.

As pretty as the girl was, he was glad to be done with her. More than glad to move on to the next youngster, who squirmed and fidgeted and talked incessantly. The kid's mouth would probably show up as a blur.

A blur was easier to explain than what he thought he'd seen when he'd taken *her* picture, in that last split-second before the shutter clicked.

A trick of the light, he told himself. Nothing more than a trick of the light.

"All right," Miss Appleton said, clapping her hands. "Timothy, quit shoving. Calvin, stop pulling Meredith's hair. And Brenda, no one wants to see your underwear, so keep your skirt down."

49

The photographer stood back, out of harm's way, as the teachers started to arrange the kids for their group photograph.

White lettering on a black background announced:

Meadowbrook Elementary School
Mr. Downs' First Grade Class
&
Miss Appleton's Second Grade Class
1988-1989

Meadowbrook Elementary was neither in sight of a meadow nor a brook, although he'd noticed there was a culvert which ran along the northern boundary of the playground. He guessed Culvert Elementary didn't have the same ring to it as Meadowbrook.

Altogether there were about forty-five children in the first and second grades—obviously overcrowded classrooms weren't a problem at this school—and it didn't take long to determine which of the children were in whose class. Miss Appleton's students, for all of her bustling efforts, were those running amok.

Mr. Downs' students were, to a child, well-behaved. They were reined in by an occasional slight frown from their teacher, who stood off to one side of the room, arms folded across his chest.

It was a safe bet that most of the second graders had been in Mr. Downs's room last year, and the photographer wondered what accounted for the marked contrast in behavior between the two classes. The different styles of their teachers?

He was far from an expert on such matters, but it appeared to him that Miss Appleton radiated uncertainty and was ill-equipped to handle her charges.

Perhaps Mr. Downs, who looked to be six foot two and a solid two hundred and fifty pounds, intimidated the devilment right out of his kids. Even a stupid kid would think twice before back-talking Goliath.

Or maybe there was a change involved in being seven years old instead of six. He vaguely recalled having heard of the terrible twos. Could there be sedate sixes and seething sevens?

Yet wasn't seven considered the age of reason, when a child could be expected to act on more than impulse? If so, he wasn't sure he wanted to know what kind of reasoning resulted in all of this frenetic activity.

The children reminded him of bees in a hive. Constant motion, but not, he thought, without purpose. He wasn't sure what, but *something* was going on here, and it made him uneasy.

He found himself searching for the girl. It didn't take long to locate her. An odd tingle went through him at the realization that she was so close by.

She stood near a window where she was back-lit by the afternoon sun. That made it difficult to see her expression, but he sensed an awareness in her, as if she knew she was being watched.

A short distance away, a tow-headed boy paid court to her, in the way that young boys had, by acting the clown. He was shadow-boxing, throwing blow after blow at an invisible opponent, bobbing and weaving all the while. Occasionally he flinched, taking a step back and covering his face with his forearms.

"Take that," the boy said, and swung wildly, the force of it pulling him off-balance. He went down to one knee. Hard.

"Kevin," a male voice said from behind the photographer. "That's enough rough-housing."

If Kevin was the boy's name he either didn't hear or chose to ignore it. He wiped his mouth and then looked at his hand wide-eyed, as if surprised to see blood. He lurched to his feet and staggered a little, moving closer to

51

the girl.

All at once the room seemed to darken, as though a cloud had passed in front of the sun.

The photographer squinted, trying to make out what was happening a few feet away.

Kevin continued towards the girl, his arms outstretched as if he intended to grab her to keep himself from falling again. His hair was damp from exertion, his shirt spotted with sweat.

The girl held her ground, raising her chin with cool defiance.

"Kevin, no!"

It happened so fast.

First, the sound, shockingly loud in a room which had gone silent.

Craaaack!

Kevin's right arm was bent at an angle that human anatomy should never allow. The bone splinters protruded from the flesh, and blood welled up before dripping onto the floor.

The boy dropped to his knees, cradling his arm to him, his color turning ashen before his eyes rolled back in his head and he slumped backwards in a faint.

The air was thick and stinging, and no one could move.

The smell of fear, the scent of blood.

Then the minute hand on the wall clock clicked and it was two straight up. A bell rang for recess, and from the hallway came the sounds of classroom doors opening and children talking and laughing.

Somehow that released them.

Mr. Downs moved to kneel by the boy's side. "Get the nurse," he said.

And although he had no idea where the nurse might be the photographer hurried out of the room to look, but not before glancing one last time at the girl.

Seven

Cheryl Appleton allowed herself to be ushered into the small supply room off the nurse's office. There was a stool near the counter but she was too agitated to sit, so she paced.

"She didn't touch him," John Downs said.

He'd closed the door but she could hear the murmur of the nurse's voice and Kevin's sniffles. The boy was only now calming down. The nurse had immobilized his arm and covered it with cold packs while they waited for the fire department ambulance to arrive.

The principal, Mr. Barry, had taken a cursory look at Kevin's arm and gone off, grim-faced, to call the boy's mother.

The memory of his shatterd arm caused the bile to rise in her throat. She wasn't good in emergencies; the tiniest drop of blood was enough to make her light-headed.

"Poor Kevin," she said. "He has to be in terrible pain."

"She didn't touch him," Downs repeated.

"I know that. I was there."

"Then don't jump to conclusions."

"I'm not. Whether she actually touched him or not, she did it to him. She broke his arm."

"Cheryl, be careful what you say."

"I don't know how she did it, I don't know why. But she did it."

"Ssh."

"Don't shush me. I'm not one of the students, and I'll say what I damned well please."

He gestured towards the closed door. "If we can hear them, they can hear us. Do you really think Kevin needs to hear this?"

"No." She stopped pacing and slumped against the counter. "No."

"Then I want you to think about this, really think about what you're suggesting, before this whole unfortunate episode gets out of hand."

"I'm thinking of that little boy in there who's trying so very hard to be brave."

"So am I."

She stared at him. "I'm not sure I believe you."

"Kevin will be fine," he said evenly. "He's a tough kid."

"Maybe he is. That isn't the point."

"Kids break bones every day—"

"*He* didn't break his arm; his arm was broken for him. There is a difference."

"Look . . . he was horsing around and he got hurt somehow. It happens."

"Why are you doing this?"

"Doing what?"

"Covering up."

He laughed. It was not a pleasant laugh. "Now you're being absurd."

"Then what do you call it?" she demanded. "You know as well as I do—"

"What do you know? What exactly did you see that *no one else* saw?"

Taken aback, Cheryl hesitated.

54

Downs answered for her: "Nothing. You saw nothing. She wasn't within two feet of him. She stood there with her arms at her sides and didn't move."

"But—"

He held up a hand. "That's all you saw because that's all there was. Kevin must have hit his arm on something, fractured the bone, and then displaced it when he was acting out."

"How could he break his arm and not know it?"

"How," he countered, "could she break his arm without anyone seeing her do it?"

"God help me, I don't know." She felt as if tentacles of ice were snaking through her veins and she shivered. "It's impossible, isn't it?"

"Yes, it is."

"Unless . . ."

"Unless what?"

She didn't know what. Perhaps, she thought uneasily, she didn't want to know. She covered her face with both hands, pressing against her closed eyelids, trying to erase the images in her mind.

Footsteps outside the door signaled the arrival of the fire department. There was a flurry of noisy activity and then, quickly it seemed, they were taking Kevin away.

"This may not be the time, and maybe I shouldn't be the one to mention it," Downs said when they'd gone, "but you *are* new here."

"What does that have to do with anything?"

He shrugged. "I understand you had some problems before you came to Meadowbrook."

"I don't know what you're referring to."

"As a student teacher?"

She felt her face redden. The principal had promised her that her teaching evaluations would remain confidential. "Who told you?"

"It wasn't Barry," he said, too quickly. "I have a friend who teaches at Hillview."

"Oh?"

"I heard you were asked to change classrooms in mid-year."

Cheryl searched his eyes. He'd spoken without a hint of censure, but she wondered. "Actually, I requested to be transferred."

"Why?"

"I'm sure if you know about my transfer, you've heard the rest of it."

"A problem with one of the students."

She let her breath out in a sigh. "Yes."

"A girl, wasn't it?"

"A girl," she acknowledged. "I gather you think I have a problem with Jill Baker."

"Don't you?"

"No."

He said nothing.

"I suppose you feel close to every one of your students," she asked, and was annoyed that she sounded defensive.

Downs shook his head. "I never said that, and I don't mean to imply that if there is a problem, you're the only one. Jill was in my class last year, and I know women have a hard time warming up to her—"

"Women?"

"She is a pretty little thing," he went on, "and although I don't see why an adult woman would be jealous of a child, they sure act that way. I mean, if she were sixteen or even thirteen I could understand that some women might feel threatened having her around."

Incredulous, unable to believe what she was hearing, Cheryl was momentarily at a loss for words.

"As for Jill, I know that she can be a bit standoffish

now and then, but kids seem to sense when someone doesn't like them. I'm sure she feels your resentment towards her and acts accordingly."

That did it. "Talk about bullshit!"

He looked affronted. "I'm not the only one who thinks so."

"I really don't give a rat's ass what you or anyone else thinks." When she was really mad, the influence of the nuns of St. Mary's gave way to the streets of Cleveland where she was raised.

"Don't take it so personally."

"I won't, as long as you don't take it personally that I think you're a jerk."

"I think you're overreacting."

"You're entitled to your opinions, however idiotic they may be, but I'm also entitled to mine." She moved past him towards the door. "And I intend to make mine known."

Eight

The bell rang at two forty-five, the same as it did every day.

Miss Appleton had not returned to the classroom after Kevin's accident so Mrs. Bastilla dismissed them. Instead of the usual rush for the door, her classmates made an orderly exit.

Jill pretended to be looking for something in her desk, waiting until they'd all gone and the halls were empty again before getting up. She gathered her books and went to her cubbyhole to get her lunchbox.

The apple she hadn't eaten at noon was rolling around in the lunchbox and rather than take it home to be recycled for tomorrow's lunch, she stopped at the wastebasket to throw it out. It thudded dully as it hit the bottom. She wrinkled her nose at the too-ripe smell.

The upper grades didn't let out until a quarter after three, and she looked in as she walked slowly past those rooms. The sixth grade class appeared to be taking a test, heads bent and furiously writing.

Jill wondered what it would take to break their concentration. Would they stay in their seats if the room became unbearably hot . . . if the paint began to boil off the walls?

59

"You'll miss your bus."

She stopped and turned, hugging her books to her.

Mr. Downs had come out of the nurse's office and was striding down the hall towards her. Even at a distance she could see the spots of blood on his shirt, dried now to a rusty brown.

"Are you okay, Jill?"

She nodded, fingering the torn cover of her math workbook. "How is Kevin?"

Mr. Downs smiled and she knew he was pleased that she'd asked. "He'll be fine. The doctors will fix his arm as good as new."

She hadn't thought about it being fixed. She lowered her head and walked on.

"They'll put a cast on it and you kids can sign your names. Then everybody will fuss over him and he won't have to do anything he doesn't want to."

"Oh."

Mr. Downs put his hand on her shoulder. "Of course, it must hurt pretty bad now."

She hoped so.

"But I don't want you to worry about that." He cupped her chin in his hand and tilted her face so he could look in her eyes. "Just . . . be a good girl."

The bus driver hadn't waited.

It made no difference; she liked walking home. The house would be empty—her mother wasn't off work till four—but she had a key to let herself in.

Sometimes there would be cookies on a plate, covered with plastic wrap. Or chocolate pudding. Or frosty cold milk.

Probably not today, though. Her mother hadn't been to the store since the weekend.

She kicked at the gravel as she crossed the school

parking lot. It clattered against the hubcaps of the teachers' cars.

Jill glanced over her shoulder to see if anyone was watching, and noticed Miss Appleton talking with Mr. Barry near the entrance to the multi-purpose room. The principal stood shaking his head as her teacher gestured.

They were too far away for their voices to carry, but she could tell that Miss Appleton was upset.

Jill stepped between two of the cars, and circled slowly to the rear. From there she could see them but they wouldn't be able to see her. Through several angles of glass they seemed even further away.

She bent down and leaned forward, resting one hand on the trunk to keep her balance.

Mr. Barry had thrust his hands in his pockets and was rocking back and forth on his heels. When her father did that, it meant he was mad.

Miss Appleton reached and touched the sleeve of his jacket. When he pulled his arm away and took a step back, she immediately closed the distance between them.

At that, he threw up his hands, as if in exasperation, then hurried off. When he got to the front of the building, he ran up the stairs, taking them two at a time, and disappeared inside.

Miss Appleton was no match for his long legs, but she followed him anyway.

What, she wondered, had made Mr. Barry mad?

She thought she knew. Something would have to be done about Miss Appleton.

But not today.

Today she was tired.

The house was stuffy from being closed up, and Jill left the front door open after making sure that the screen door was locked. She picked up the mail that had been dropped through the slot and carried it with her into the kitchen.

After putting the mail on the table, she went to the refrigerator to look for a snack.

All she could find was a can of Hershey's Fudge Topping. She took off the yellow plastic lid and used her finger to get a taste.

The rich, slightly bitter flavor was just what she needed to quell her hunger.

She went to get a spoon.

Nine

Georgia fixed spaghetti for dinner, going to the trouble of shaping individual meatballs rather than simply frying the hamburger and dumping it in the sauce, but Jill ate only a few bites before asking to be excused.

"Aren't you feeling well?" Spaghetti was usually a favorite.

"I'm not hungry."

Georgia frowned, put down her fork and wiped her hands on her napkin. "Come here, honey."

Jill pushed her chair away from the table and came around to stand by her side.

"You look a little flushed," Georgia said. She placed the palm of her hand on her daughter's forehead, but although her color was high, the child's skin was cool and dry to the touch. "Well, you don't seem to have a fever."

"I'm okay."

"Hmm." Georgia smoothed the hair back from Jill's face, tucking the silken strands behind her ears. "Then you're excused."

Jill went to take her plate to the sink.

"But put on your slippers," Georgia said, belatedly

noticing that the girl was barefoot. "I don't want you catching cold."

She finished her own dinner and started to clean up, scraping the remains off Jill's plate into the disposal. She flipped the switch and listened to it grind, standing to one side so that if the motor decided to seize up, she wouldn't get the back flow in her face.

It took the disposal forever and a day to devour the spaghetti, but she couldn't throw it in the garbage.

In the past few weeks, the neighborhood had been plagued with dogs. No one knew where they'd come from, but there were packs of them, lean hungry-looking animals, and they got into the trash cans at night, scrounging for whatever they could find.

She didn't want the smell of food attracting them into the yard, especially now that they had Hoppity.

All of which reminded her that the town council had agreed to a meeting early next week to discuss what they could do about the dogs and she wanted to call a few of her neighbors to organize a committee.

Of course, it was the dinner hour, not the best time to be knocking on doors.

Dinner hour. How long had it been since they'd had an old-fashioned family dinner? How long since Dave had even had dinner at home?

Maybe she and Jill should go down to the restaurant some night and surprise him.

For some reason, the prospect made her uncomfortable.

She ran hot water, intending to let the dishes soak. As she waited for the sink to fill, she glanced out the kitchen window at the house across the street and was surprised to see the porch light on.

The doctor was in town, then.

Should she invite him to the meeting? Maybe he wouldn't want to be bothered; although he'd bought the house some five years ago, he was seldom there.

From what others had told her, he lived and worked in Los Angeles. Every few months he showed up in Winslow and spent a day or two at the house.

Georgia had a nodding acquaintance with him, but they'd never spoken. He kept to himself, mostly, but he always had a smile for Jill.

He had a nice smile.

It wouldn't do any harm to ask, she decided. As a doctor, he was probably more interested than most in matters of public health and safety.

But when she knocked on his door there was no answer. On the chance that he was upstairs or on the phone, she knocked again and waited, pulling her sweater around her to ward off the evening breeze.

She leaned forward, listening for any signs of movement inside, but heard nothing. There were glass panes on either side of the door, and she had to resist the urge to peek into the house.

"That you, Georgia?"

Georgia turned. "Oh hello, Mr. Rafferty." Old Rafferty—no one seemed to know his given name—was the neighborhood curmudgeon. Even though he wore half-inch thick glasses, carried a cane, and claimed to be legally blind, there wasn't much that got by him.

"He's not home," Rafferty said.

"But he is in town?"

"Yup."

Feeling awkward at having been caught with her ear to the door—a minute later and her face might have been pressed to the window—she moved to join the old man on the street. Even in the open air, he smelled of mothballs and of the anise cookies that were his passion.

"How are you?" she asked.

He waved the question off. "Same, the same. Nothing wrong, is there?"

"What?"

"You got somebody sick at home? Needing a doctor?"

"No, no." She looked back at the house. "I thought I'd ask him if he'd like to be on the neighborhood committee we're forming. About the dogs."

"Dogs." Rafferty swept the air with his cane. "They ought to shoot 'em."

She inclined her head slightly but said nothing; he could interpret that however he wanted.

"Or they could try sprinkling arsenic in a garbage can or two."

Georgia knew he was trying to get a rise out of her and that if she took the bait, he'd keep her here arguing half the night, but she couldn't let that pass. "I hope you're not serious—"

"But whatever they do," he went on as if she hadn't spoken, "what makes you think a big city doctor would give a fig about our little problems?"

"He lives here, too."

"That depends on your point of view."

"I suppose it does. I just thought . . . well, never mind. I'd better get back to the house. Jill will be wondering where I am." She smiled to be polite and turned to go. "Goodnight, Mr. Rafferty."

"Mind you, I think you're wasting your time," Rafferty called after her. "But you probably can reach him at the hospital if you want to try . . ."

Jill was asleep when Georgia went in to check on her, curled up on top of the bed in her flannel pajamas and pink slippers.

66

"So much for having someone keep me company tonight," she said under her breath. She covered Jill with an afghan and reached to turn out the lamp, then remembered.

Where were the buttons?

They weren't on the bedside table where she'd told Jill to leave them. Carefully, quietly, she opened the drawer to look for them, but the only items she saw were hair ribbons, pencils, paper clips, rubber bands, and several broken crayons.

At that moment, Jill sighed in her sleep. Her eyelashes fluttered—was she dreaming?—and her mouth formed a perfect pout.

Georgia smiled.

Not wanting to wake her, Georgia closed the drawer and turned off the light.

"Sweet dreams," she whispered.

For awhile she busied herself around the house, picking up and putting things away, but she lost interest when she realized that by doing so, she was revealing how much dust had built up since her last cleaning.

Intending to settle in for a night of watching TV, she went first to the kitchen to get a soft drink and rediscovered the mail.

Bills.

There were always bills.

The MasterCard bill was higher than she'd expected, but Dave had a nasty habit of losing the charge slips, or leaving them in a shirt pocket to disintegrate in the wash.

"The wash! Damn."

The clothes were still out on the line; she'd forgotten entirely. Again.

It was fully dark out and Georgia got the flashlight

from the junk drawer before heading out the back door. It slammed behind her, startling something which rustled in the bushes.

She didn't turn the light on the bushes, because no matter what was there, she'd rather not know. Any creature which preferred a nocturnal lifestyle was not one she cared to see.

Georgia crossed the yard.

She'd always loved the smell of clothes hung out to dry in the fresh air, and she breathed in the clean scent as she gathered them in her arms. They were a little damp in the corners, but spring was still something of an illusion; the afternoons were chilly despite the clear blue skies they'd been having.

She shoved a handful of wooden clothespins into her jeans pocket, and turned to go into the house, hugging the clothes to her and pointing the flashlight so she could see where she was stepping. Some of the flat oval stones that Dave had used to create a walkway had worked loose from all the rain they'd had this past winter, but he was too busy nowadays to be fixing things around the house.

The restaurant was taking more of his time than either of them had anticipated in the beginning, but, as he never failed to point out, it had been her idea that they start a business of their own.

"I'm doing this for you and Jill," he'd say. "You know what they say tuitions will be running by the time Jill is ready for college."

Her foot skidded and slipped off a stepping stone, and into the surrounding mud.

"Great." She pulled her foot loose and pointed the light at her shoe; an inch of mud caked the heel. At least these weren't her new Reeboks.

She stamped her shoe but the mud clung. Of course, it *would* cling, right up until the moment she stepped into the house. Then she could track it through the kitchen and spend the rest of the evening mopping up.

"Wonderful," she said.

As if in response to her voice, something stirred behind her and she whirled.

Everything was still.

A few feet away, she could see the dark shape of the rabbit hutch by the elm tree, and she wondered if she should ask Dave to move it closer to the house, where Hoppity would be safer. It'd take him all of five minutes . . .

Five minutes or five hours, he'd be annoyed, and he wouldn't bother to hide how he felt. Why, he'd want to know, hadn't she thought about such things when the man from the pet shop had delivered it?

Why indeed?

Jill hadn't been as excited about her Easter present as Georgia imagined she would be.

Dave was sure to remind her that they could ill afford the money she'd spent.

And the rabbit, named Hoppity not by acclamation but by default—Jill steadfastly refusing to voice a preference—had been pretty much ignored, the poor thing.

Georgia sighed and frowned, dragging the heel of her shoe through the thick grass.

The sleeve of one of Dave's shirts brushing the ground and she lifted it clear, tucking it back into the bundle. As she did so, the flashlight beam showed Hoppity huddled in the corner of his hutch. Were rabbits scared of the dark, too?

"I know how you feel," she said to him. And muddy shoes or not, she hurried back inside.

Friday

Ten

The biggest difference, Noah Huston felt, between small towns and big cities was that small towns could be so quiet, and it was the silence that awoke him.

In Los Angeles, no matter what the hour, there was noise: speeding motorcycles, trucks lumbering by, mufflerless cars, and the unnerving sound of helicopters passing overhead.

And sirens.

Sirens always woke him, perhaps because he was a doctor—Pavlov's dog responding to a different kind of bell?—but now the absence of sirens had brought him from sleep.

It wasn't light out yet, and he glanced at the clock. Five forty-five.

Too damn early.

He closed his eyes experimentally, on the chance that he might doze off, but that only magnified his awareness that not even the crickets were stirring. He found himself listening for the settling sounds that houses made, or the low hum of the refrigerator.

Nothing.

It occurred to him that the fog which had been descending on the town as he'd driven home late last night had thickened into a dense cocoon through which nothing could be heard. He imagined it enveloping the house, tendrils of mist probing for points of entry . . .

"Uh huh," he said, and sat up in bed. He shook his head to clear it. What was it about this place that invited such surreal ruminations?

Winslow was a small town very much like other small towns he'd seen, with modest homes, an unobtrusive business community, and a largely indetectable infrastructure. A majority of the residents were of retirement age—he had a suspicion that Winslow might not exist if not for the senior citizens and their social security benefits and pensions—but there were also families with school-age children.

The town had a single elementary school which offered classes for kindergarten through the sixth grade, but shared the secondary school with its closest neighbor, aptly named Tranquility.

Some of the residents commuted to jobs in the larger surrounding towns, but by and large, most worked in Winslow. Living was slow and, if not exactly easy, it wasn't as hard as the city. People smiled.

By day, there was nothing of the gothic about Winslow, and yet . . .

No, it wasn't the town.

It was her.

After arriving in Winslow, he'd spent most of the afternoon and all evening at the small Community Hospital which served the town. Since he held a high advisory position in the physicians' group that supplied the doctors who staffed the hospital's tiny emergency room, he pretty much had the run of the place.

As usual, he began by reviewing admissions records, looking for patterns, but also for anything out of the ordinary.

With the town's elderly population, most admissions were to be expected: myocardial infarctions, unstable angina, congestive heart failure, pneumonia, chronic obstructive pulmonary disease, and the like.

Surgical procedures were rare—the facilities were adequate but surgeons preferred to admit their patients to larger hospitals than Community—but there was the occasional appendectomy, excisions of basal cell carcinoma or ganglion cysts.

Among younger patients, tonsillectomy and adnoidectomy were the most frequently performed surgeries, followed closely by bilateral myringotomy for chronic acute otitis media.

None of which was of interest to him.

The traumas were what he was looking for. Accidents, particularly those involving children.

More specifically, accidents without a clear and obvious cause.

A child on a skateboard could be expected to get hurt sooner or later. Kids routinely fell off jungle gyms, they bumped heads while engaging in horseplay, they skinned their knees and elbows roller skating, they sprained ankles playing soccer or baseball or other games.

A child doing none of these things, a child playing quietly in a schoolyard, for example, might be considered to be reasonably safe.

Not in this town.

In Winslow, kids got hurt doing nothing at all.

In the years he'd been searching through the records, he'd found a number of these inexplicable instances, most resulting in minor injuries, abrasions and contusions, sprains, a rare fracture now and then.

The medical records of those children revealed certain similarities.

First, they were all between the ages of five and eleven.

75

Naturally—there being no alternative—they were students at Meadowbrook Elementary. Not so naturally, eighty percent of the injuries occurred on the school grounds.

All maintained they were "not doing anything" when injured.

Most were boys, at a ratio of three to one.

All had abnormally low pulse rates when first seen in the emergency room.

All showed sluggish reflexes, and slowed neurological responses for at least an hour after being injured. Eye exams revealed that their pupils were not adequately reactive to light.

In most instances, the medical personnel had ascribed these abnormalities to a form of shock, although at least one doctor had ordered a drug screen when an eight-year-old boy had a mild seizure after suffering a dislocated right shoulder while at school.

"Rule out ingestion of unknown substance," the doctor had written.

Huston had sought out the doctor involved, finally reaching her by phone. But although she knew immediately to which case he was referring, she had no answer for him.

"It was odd," she'd told him, "I wasn't sure *what* was going on with him. He had no history of seizures, no known head injury. I kept him for observation and his condition improved. That's all I can say."

"What about your impressions."

"I've just said—"

"Not medically. Emotionally. What made you suspect drugs?"

For a moment she'd been silent. In the background he heard a beeper go off. "Listen, I've got to call my service—"

"Please."

"I don't know," she sighed. "These days an eight-year-old on drugs isn't uncommon."

"In LA, maybe."

"Even in the small towns. He just looked drugged to me. Hell, he looked anesthetized. Or hypnotized."

Yes, he thought.

"And to be honest, I was covering my ass. Defensive medicine, you understand?"

He understood.

Then yesterday afternoon, after all the years he'd been coming to Winslow, he'd had a chance to see first-hand what he'd only read about.

They'd brought in Kevin Browne, age seven, with a compound fracture of the right radius and ulna. The boy was unable to talk, nearly stuporous, but the fire department medic related a history of non-traumatic injury.

"The teacher said he was just standing there and all of a sudden his arm broke."

And Huston knew he had one.

He could track this injury back to its cause.

As much as he wanted to remain objective, he already knew what he'd find.

Jill.

He showered and dressed, then went to the kitchen to put on a pot of coffee. He'd bought a couple of apple Danish at the bakery in town, and he warmed one in the microwave, trying not to think about what his patients would say if they saw him indulging in the pastries he'd warned them to give up.

It was still early, not yet seven a.m., so he relaxed, having two cups of black coffee and finishing the Danish before going to the front room to take his position.

He drew back the drapes and the morning sunlight

flooded the room. The fog had dissipated, and the sky was a crisp blue.

The child wouldn't be leaving for school for awhile, but he was prepared to sit and wait.

He didn't want to miss her. Not when so much was at stake

Eleven

Georgia went out in her bathrobe to get the paper, breathing in the fresh, sweet air. The grass was damp— last night's fog had been the worst yet—but the sun promised warmth for later.

It was going to be a beautiful day.

She returned to the house and took the paper with her into the front room to read while having her tea, but then found herself putting it aside. The morning was too perfect to spoil with news of this or that tragedy, and that was all the newspapers seemed to print of late.

Even the local *Winslow Gazette* went out of its way to import bad news, reporting on drug busts, gang warfare and the almost nightly drive-by shootings that plagued Los Angeles. It made her anxious for her sister Beverly. And Katy, who at eight could hardly be expected to understand the violence around her.

Georgia sighed and shook her head. She really didn't want to think about any of that. She took a sip of tea and contemplated the day ahead of her. If only it would stay this peaceful.

And it *was* blissfully peaceful. She supposed that she should feel guilty about it, but early morning had come to be her favorite time of day, those hours before Dave or

Jill were awake.

It wasn't that she wanted the house to herself—in fact she was alone more often than she cared to be—but rather in the morning her world felt safer than at any other time. She could walk through the quiet rooms and enjoy her solitude without having to worry that somewhere, one of them might be needing her.

Knowing where they were comforted her.

She didn't consider herself an over-protective mother, but since the first day of kindergarten, she'd been nervous about Jill.

Perhaps it was because Jill was adopted, but she'd never been able to shake the feeling that the child could be taken away. It was as if, since she hadn't endured the pain to bring her daughter into the world, she had no real claim to her.

Legal papers weren't the same as the bond of shared blood.

What if someday, Jill's natural mother showed up on their doorstep?

The law, she knew, was on her side, but despite centuries of trying, man still wasn't able to legislate feelings, to control human emotion. A child couldn't be forced to love.

Georgia frowned.

Jill was fine. She might not be as demonstrative as other children, but Georgia attributed that to the fact that she'd been without a real family for the first year of her life.

Even now, it upset her that her poor baby had been shunted from home to home. What possessed those people to reject an innocent child? Had they no heart?

If only she and Dave had been the first.

Dave.

He hadn't come home yet when she went to bed at eleven. Nor was he in when she woke shortly after one.

She'd gotten up and stood at the window, thinking she'd heard a car. She couldn't see through the fog, but she stayed there, shivering from the cold, willing him home.

Finally, a pair of headlights turned onto the street, but it was only the doctor.

She'd gone back to bed then.

Sometime during the night, Dave apparently tiptoed in, undressed, and crawled into bed beside her. He was sleeping with his back to her when the alarm went off at six, oblivious to the sound.

When she looked to see that he was all right, she noticed the smile on his face.

Dreaming about what?

The teacup rattled as she put it on the saucer, and she realized that her hands were shaking.

Annoyed at the turn her thoughts had taken, she got up and went into the kitchen to start breakfast.

While Dave was in the shower and Jill ate her breakfast, Georgia went into the bedroom. She took the vacation fund piggybank off the dresser and sat on the bed.

She turned the bank upside down and used a butter knife to guide the coins out the narrow opening.

A nickel, a dime, another nickel.

It was slow going, but she needed enough to give to Jill so that she could buy lunch at school. Normally Jill turned her nose up at cafeteria food, but today, as befitting the day before a holiday, there was a special menu, a choice of hamburgers or hotdogs, with potato chips, fresh fruit, and ice cream bars.

Overall, the food represented a nutritional wasteland, but there probably wasn't a child at Meadowbrook who could resist it.

And it saved her from having to make lunch.

"Ah ha," she said as a quarter dropped out. "Come to Mama."

Three pennies tried to come through the slot at the same time and became wedged. She turned the bank right side up and forced them back inside.

"I haven't got all day," she told the pig sternly, and shook him for luck. She was rewarded with another quarter and two dimes.

Thank heavens today was payday at the Library. On her break she would make a deposit to cover the checks she'd mailed yesterday, and hold out enough cash to pay for her own meals next week, Easter week.

It was too bad she wouldn't be able to take time off from work like she had last year, but they needed the money. She hated to leave Jill alone, but she didn't have a choice, really.

At least she worked nearby. If Jill needed her, she could be home in minutes.

A dime and a penny slid along the knife blade and dropped onto the other coins. She poked at them, counting. "Seventy-six cents."

The school lunch was a dollar fifty, and extra ice cream bars were priced at twenty-five cents. Another dollar and Jill could have it all.

Her gaze turned to the chair by the dresser where Dave had draped his pants. She could see a corner of his wallet and a thin edge of green within it.

Would he even know if she borrowed a dollar?

The piggybank was heavy in her hands, full of change. It wouldn't take *that* long to get the rest of the money, she thought, but it would be easier to use a bill.

On the other hand, she had never taken money from her husband's wallet. He'd never told her not to, but her own mother had been an alcoholic who regularly snuck money from her father's billfold to pay for her booze, and she'd always felt that doing so was wrong.

Of course, paying for their daughter's lunch was something else entirely.

At that moment the water in the shower turned off and she glanced at the bathroom door. She heard the shower curtain being drawn back.

She put the piggybank on the bed and got up, moving without sound to the chair. The wallet fit snugly in the pocket, but she pulled it free.

Georgia took a breath and opened it, listening at the same time for footsteps nearing the door.

He had a twenty, a five and three singles.

With her fingertips, she eased one of the singles out of the wallet.

Now put it back, she thought.

Her heart had begun to pound.

Put it back.

Her hands refused to do as she bid them, but rather they opened the wallet wider, and began to finger through the folded slips of paper tucked inside. There were a surprising number of them, she thought.

"What are you looking for?" she asked herself.

From behind the bathroom door, the medicine cabinet squeaked open, startling her.

That was enough. She closed the wallet and shoved it back in his pants pocket.

After replacing the piggybank on the dresser, she scooped up the coins and left the room hurriedly.

She didn't want to be there when Dave came out of the bathroom.

Georgia stood inside the front door, watching as Jill walked down the street to the corner where the other children were waiting for the school bus.

Jill stopped a short distance from where they were gathered, and it seemed to Georgia that the other kids moved back. The animation that they'd displayed before Jill arrived was markedly absent.

It was a scene she'd witnessed before, she realized.

Other children didn't take to Jill.

Georgia felt an ache in her heart at the sight of her daughter standing alone.

Twelve

Roland Barry arrived at Meadowbrook Elementary at precisely seven-thirty as he'd been doing since being named principal more than two years before. He parked in his reserved space and was gratified to see that, as usual, he was the first to arrive.

He unlocked the front doors and stepped inside, pausing for a moment to admire the serenity and even beauty of the empty hall. It wouldn't stay this way long, but the night custodian had done a nifty job on the floors, buffing the hardwood to a warm glow.

All along the hall the doors were shut, the classrooms dark and silent.

The building smelled strongly of chalk and pencil shavings, and it evoked nostalgia in him for his own school days, many years ago.

Schoolhouses like this were the reason why he'd gone into education.

Life never got any better.

His footsteps echoed most satisfactorily as he walked to the office and let himself in. After turning on the lights at the master panel, he went into his office and put his briefcase on the desk.

85

His desk was clear except for an inter-office envelope which was resting face down on the blotter, centered in Lucy Chisolm's distinctive fashion.

A strip of Scotch tape covered the point of the flap. Beneath the tape was a black smudged fingerprint: she'd been changing the ribbon on her massive old IBM typewriter when he'd left for the day.

He frowned.

Sealed envelopes seldom held good news, but beyond that, if Lucy had information she felt was sensitive enough to justify being delivered in this way, why hadn't she contacted him at home with it?

She knew how much he disliked being greeted by a crisis before he'd had a chance to make his rounds and get his bearings.

Irritated, he snatched the envelope off the desk and carried it with him as he pursued his routine, going to open the venetian blinds. It took a moment or two of fiddling before the blinds were adjusted to his taste, and then he stood as he did every morning, looking out on the school grounds, surveying his domain, but of course now it wasn't the same.

He was uncomfortably aware of the weight of the envelope in his hand.

Trying to ignore it, he squinted at the trees and considered whether they should be trimmed. Yes, he decided, although they looked the same as they had the day before—and the day before that.

One could never be too careful with trees, he believed. They weren't to be trusted; the damn things could actually go and die, and still remain standing, in a kind of reverse game of possum:

I'm dead but I look alive.

In addition, they developed root rot, housed termites, or became infested with repulsively ugly beetles. They oozed sap—tree blood—that could take the paint off a car.

Limbs as thick as a man's waist could splinter into kindling under the weight of a first grader, dashing the child to the ground. That very thing had happened the first week of school.

The child had broken his wrist.

Chances were, the news of the latest school mishap was what waited within the envelope he held. Mr. Barry tightened his grip on it, not caring at all that it wrinkled in his hand.

There was no avoiding it, he realized.

He peeled the tape off the flap of the envelope and opened it. Two sheets of paper, one white, one yellow, were folded accordian-style inside.

"In duplicate, yet," he said, taking them out.

As he'd feared, the letter from Lucy detailed the report the hospital had given her on the injury the Browne boy had received.

Compound fracture of the right radius and ulna. Translated: a badly broken arm.

Well, he'd known that—one look at the boy's arm was enough to convince him—but apparently it was worse than even the medics had suspected. Surgery was necessary, and the boy was transferred today to the county hospital in Leland where the fracture would be stabilized by "internal fixation" of the bones.

He'd gained some expertise in medical terminology in his years here, and knew this meant they were going to put metal pins in the child's arm.

A very bad break indeed.

For the boy *and* the school.

His ulcer threatened to act up as he read further down the page.

Cheryl Appleton wanted to see him during morning

recess, or she would "take action" on her own.

"Lord save me," he said. He'd listened to more than he'd wanted of her crazy accusations yesterday, and put it down to female hysteria.

And what had she really had to say? That little Jill Baker had broken her classmate's arm.

Right. As if a delicate child like Jill could even do such a thing. All anyone had to do was look at that pretty face and know better.

The only thing the girl would ever break was male hearts.

Hearing that nonsense from Miss Appleton, he'd wondered if John Downs was right. Downs had a theory for everything, and this theory proposed that ordinary females would always denigrate extraordinary females.

Weren't the women who protested beauty pageants less attractive than the contestants?

But, although he'd been sorely tempted, he hadn't accused her of being jealous of the child. Instead he'd walked away.

According to Lucy's letter, the second grade teacher had left the school in tears after he'd barricaded himself in his office. She had later called to request the meeting, and had hinted that her attorney might be present.

Well, she'd had all night to sleep on it, and he could only hope that she'd come to her senses by now.

Otherwise it was going to be a long day.

He scanned the remainder of the page, grunting as he noted that Lucy had sent flowers to the boy in the hospital in the school's and his name—a nice gesture although flowers alone wouldn't necessarily keep the Brownes from suing—and that she'd reported the injury to the school's insurance carrier.

So . . . all he had to do was defuse the ticking bomb

Miss Appleton was sure to throw at him.

He folded the letter and returned it to the envelope, which he then tucked in his inside jacket pocket.

Forewarned is forearmed, he thought, and went to start his rounds.

As luck would have it, he ran into Cheryl Appleton as he was crossing the parking lot.

"Mr. Barry," she said, hurrying to catch up to him. "May I talk to you?"

He smiled and cocked his head, he hoped disarmingly. "I really haven't the time now."

"It's important." She fell in step beside him as though he hadn't spoken. "I know you think I was just upset yesterday—"

"As anyone would be."

"But it's more than that."

Not wanting to encourage her, he said nothing.

"I would have to be blind not to see what's been going on here."

"Oh?"

"And you must have seen it as well."

He felt a flash of annoyance. He didn't care to be told what he must see by a superior, much less a *teacher*. "I have no idea what you're referring to."

She grabbed his arm, stopping him in his tracks and making him face her.

"I don't believe you."

"Miss Appleton," he said, "may I advise you that you're dangerously close to insubordination?"

She surprised him by laughing and he noticed that her eyes were glittering. What fires were raging in her mind? he wondered.

"I think you'd better go to your classroom." He

removed her hand from his person. "The buses are starting to arrive and I'm sure you have things to do before the school day starts."

"You're not going to listen to me, are you?"

"Not when you're so clearly having emotional distress." He saw that her mouth had begun to tremble and felt that he had gained control. "To be honest, it hasn't escaped my attention that you've been having a lot of trouble handling your class. Now that I think of it, it might be best for everyone if you took a sick day."

"But I'm not sick," she protested.

There was a hesitancy in her voice that hadn't been there before and he pressed his advantage. "I insist. As your principal, I would be remiss in my duties to both you and the children if I allowed you to go into that room in your . . . condition."

Her eyes closed and she lowered her head. "Please let me stay."

"I'm sorry, no." Oddly, now that he had beaten her, he *was* sorry. "We've a week's vacation from school, and I'm sure the time off will make a new woman of you."

Without another word, he walked away.

He had nearly reached the trees when he heard the screech of tires.

In the split second it took him to turn, he imagined the worst—a bus plowing into a crowd of kids—and so he felt a measure of relief when there was but a single person in the vehicle's path.

Miss Appleton.

What was she doing standing there?

The bus struck her a glancing blow, but it was enough to send her flying through the air. She landed on the steps of the school, knocking down a red-haired little girl who immediately began to cry.

Several yards away, Jill Baker collapsed to the ground in a faint.

When his joints unfroze, Mr. Barry began to run towards the school.

Thirteen

The Winslow Library was bereft of patrons and Georgia busied herself going through the returned books and erasing the margin notes that some of the more opinionated book-borrowers had made.

Most of the notations were innocuous corrections of typographical errors, but some were rather testy asides, apparently meant to talk back to the author, or, she supposed, to alert the future readers of the book to its inadequacies.

A few were obscene.

"What are you smiling about?" Faye Paxton asked as she pushed the book cart to the check-out counter.

"Someone in this town is a pervert."

"Just one? That's a disappointment."

Georgia shook her head and kept erasing. "Don't be. This is a world–class pervert."

"Oh? Let me see."

"Never mind." She flipped through the pages of the book, scanning for further notations. The pervert had used a red pencil to make sure his or her comments would be noticed.

As if anyone could ignore them.

"Speaking of the sexually imaginative," Faye said,

lowering her voice although there was no one to overhear, "did you happen to notice yesterday that little Brucie Shaw was spending a lot of time thumbing through those paperback bodice-rippers?"

"Was he?"

"Was he ever." Faye took the books Georgia was finished with and put them on the cart. "It used to be that the male adventure books had the hot stuff, but these days it's the romance novels that'll steam your clams."

"Faye!"

"It's true. But my point was, kids start at a younger age than you and I did."

Georgia lifted an eyebrow.

"Well, maybe not me. But he's what? Eleven?"

"Ten."

Faye opened the book Georgia had just finished with. "Ten years old and already hot-blooded. Doesn't that bother you?"

"Why should it bother me? I'm not his mother."

"But you have a daughter."

Georgia felt a tingle of apprehension and she frowned. All at once she had the strongest feeling that something was wrong.

"What is it, Georgia? What's wrong?" Faye asked, reaching across the counter to touch her hand. "You look as though you've seen a ghost."

"I don't know."

"Are you feeling all right?"

"Yes, I'm—" But she couldn't go on. Her mind was racing, but somehow her mouth refused to form the words she wanted to say.

"Maybe you should go in the back and rest for a minute," Faye suggested.

Georgia nodded mutely.

*   *   *

There wasn't a couch, but Faye helped Georgia to the only comfortable chair in the library, an overstuffed monstrosity that had been around for longer than anyone could remember.

Georgia sank into the cushions and it seemed to swallow her up.

"Let me get you a glass of water," Faye said when she was settled, and crossed to the water fountain. She took a Dixie cup and filled it. In her haste, she spilled some on the floor.

Georgia took a sip. "Thank you," she whispered, finding her voice.

"Should I call a doctor?"

Despite her sudden malaise, she knew that it wasn't she who was ill. "No, but—"

"Dave? You want me to call Dave?"

She shook her head. "The school. Call Jill's school."

"The school, okay." Faye hurried across the room, nearly slipping in the water. When she'd reached the phone she turned and faced Georgia, her expression doubtful. "Why am I calling the school?"

"I think something's happened to Jill."

"The line's still busy," Faye reported and hung up the phone.

"Keep trying, would you?"

"Sure."

Georgia watched as Faye punched out the number for what had to be the twentieth time. Even from where she sat she could hear the drone of the busy signal. "Call the operator," she suggested. "Tell them it's an emergency; they can break in on the line."

"An emergency. What if they ask what kind of an emergency?"

"They won't. Please, Faye."

Faye depressed the switchhook. "If it'll make you feel better—"

"What's that?"

"What?"

"Don't you hear that?" Georgia concentrated on the sound. "A siren."

Faye's brow furrowed. "I don't hear anything."

"It's getting closer—"

"Hold on." Faye held a hand up to stop her. "The line is ringing. Damn. You'd think the operator would answer faster than this."

Georgie sat forward, her hands gripping the arms of the chair. "Do you hear it?"

"Yes, but it doesn't mean that it's for Jill. I mean, this town is full of old people . . . oh, hello?"

She got to her feet and stood for a moment, waiting for the dizziness to pass, then left the office, ignoring Faye's pantomimed objections and went straight to the door which faced the street.

There was nothing to see—several streets separated the library from the school—but she was able to tell that the ambulance had gone in that direction.

Just then the siren cut off in mid-wail.

Georgia had taken a few steps, thinking that she could cut across people's yards and reach the school faster than if she drove, when Faye caught her arm from behind.

"Georgia," she said, "the operator couldn't get through. It seems as if all the lines are on hold. None of the people who are waiting on hold are willing to give up their lines, but even if they were, it appears that no one at the school is answering the calls."

"Something dreadful must have happened."

"Not necessarily—"

"I'm going to the school."

Faye held onto her. "How? You can't drive a car the way you're feeling right now; you can barely stand on your own."

"Then you take me."

"But the library . . ."

"Lock it up. Put a sign on the door." She gripped Faye's hand. "She's all I have."

Faye's lips parted in surprise.

"Do you hear me?"

"Yes, I hear you. Go wait for me by my car."

But when they arrived at the school, the ambulance had already gone.

A cluster of children were being waved into the building by Mrs. Chisolm, the school secretary. Several were crying but others were bright-eyed with curiosity.

Georgia searched every face, not finding Jill's.

Mrs. Chisolm shepherded the stragglers through the double doors. When she turned, her expression grew serious. She walked heavily down the steps to where Georgia stood by the curb.

"You're Jill's mother, aren't you?"

"Yes."

"Now Mrs. Baker, I don't want you to worry—"

"What's happened to her?"

"Not a thing. She just fainted."

But Georgia had spotted bloodstains on the pavement and she pointed to them wordlessly. If she'd fainted, had she hit her head?

"Really, Mrs. Baker, I wouldn't lie to you."

"But the blood . . ."

"It isn't Jill's. One of the teachers was injured here this morning."

Georgia nodded, but in fact the words had fled her mind instantaneously. "Where is my daughter? I want to see Jill."

"Well, they've taken her to the hospital."

That she heard. "I thought you said—"

"As a precaution. To check her out. She was conscious and alert, and I'm sure she'll be fine."

Faye, who'd been standing in the opened door of her car, looking over the roof at them, slapped her palm on the metal. "Come on, Georgia. I can get you to the hospital in ten minutes flat."

They made it in seven.

Fourteen

"I know it hurts, but I want you to take a deep breath and hold it . . ."

Cheryl Appleton drew a breath as instructed and felt hot stabbing pains all along the left side of her ribcage. "Oh!"

"Hold it, hold it. Don't move."

The x-ray machine made a whirring sound and somewhere in the background she heard a click. The pain radiated down her side where it joined a duller throbbing in her hip. Tears formed in her eyes and she blinked.

"Great, good job."

She took that to mean she could release the air in her lungs. Exhaling hurt less than inhaling, but it was not without drawbacks: she could feel the bones scraping against each other.

The lead-aproned radiology technician came from around the divider. "Just relax for a few minutes, while I run this through the developer. We want to make sure we've got a clean shot."

He disappeared before she could respond.

Relax, she thought. As if she could. The x-ray table was incredibly hard and cold, and she'd been laying here for what must have been hours.

Every muscle in her body ached, and the skinned areas on her left leg, hip, elbow and shoulder where she'd landed on the pavement burned. A nurse had cleaned them with an orange-colored antiseptic which supposedly didn't sting.

Cheryl had news for them. It stung.

In addition, her head felt as if it were full of cotton candy, some of which had thickened her tongue. Her mouth tasted of blood.

There was a clock on the wall that she could see if she turned her head, and when the technician did not return, she made the effort. The second hand swept around, and minutes passed.

Fifteen minutes.

Twenty.

"Hello?" she called when she couldn't take anymore. "Is anyone there?"

No one answered.

Cheryl had to fight her panic. She was helpless; how would she ever get down from the table on her own? And even if she could, if she didn't fall in the attempt, would she be able to stand?

What if her movements forced a sharp-edged bone—and she knew her ribs were broken—into an artery or into her heart? Might that happen? Anatomy hadn't been one of her better subjects, but she thought there were a lot of vital organs at risk.

But then, wasn't she already at risk, having been left unattended?

With that thought in mind, and despite her protesting ribs, she carefully drew in as much air as her lungs would allow, intending to yell.

It came out as more of a whimper: "Help me."

"What is it, dear?"

The voice was male, sounded older, and had come from a part of the room she couldn't see. It definitely didn't belong to the technician who'd been there earlier. "Will you . . . help me?"

"What's wrong?"

She could only manage two words at a time. "I've been here . . . a long . . . time. I hurt . . . bad. I'm having . . . a lot of . . . pain. Can you . . . help me?"

"I'm not sure," the man said. "I'm only a volunteer."

He came into her view and peered at her through thick black-rimmed glasses. He wore a pink smock and his name tag read M. Rafferty.

To her, he resembled an angel.

"Mister . . . Rafferty. Would you call a . . . nurse?"

"Sure will."

She closed her eyes in relief. "Thank you."

An eternity later, one of the emergency room nurses and an orderly came into the room and without saying anything to her, pushed a gurney next to the x-ray table.

The discomfort of laying on its hard surface combined with the effort she'd expended telling the volunteer of her plight had drained her. She didn't have the energy to be brave anymore and screamed with pain when they shifted her from the table onto the gurney.

"Where are the x-rays?" the nurse asked the technician who had silently reappeared, apparently in response to her screams.

"I already sent them to ER."

"And kept the patient?" She smoothed the sheet over Cheryl and pulled up a loose-weaved blanket. "I think it's customary to return the patient *with* the films."

"You know Dr. Costa. If he doesn't like the quality of the films, he'll send her right back for more."

"Well then, did you at least *tell* someone the films were ready? I don't think the doctor's even looked at them."

"I didn't tell anyone, because I messengered them

101

down. Ask the volunteer who brought them."

"Half the old coots who work here are senile," the nurse said and finally shoved the gurney in the direction of the door. "Next time tell someone who's got something on the ball."

"And where would I find someone like that?" the technician retorted. "I mean, in this place?"

The orderly laughed and was rewarded with a dirty look from the nurse. "Don't encourage him."

At last.

Cheryl never thought that lying on her back watching the ceiling pass by would be the high point of her day, but it was. Dr. Costa was waiting in the emergency room for her, and now that she'd been x-rayed, he would give her something for the pain.

He'd promised.

She had always been the kind of person who refused an offer of aspirin for a headache, proud of herself for dealing with her discomfort without resorting to drugs. Now she'd gladly get down on her knees and beg for medication, pride be damned.

As they passed through a maze of corridors she became aware of a prickly sensation in the heels of both feet. The circulation was returning to them after they'd been numbed by the unforgiving surface of the x-ray table.

It was not a pleasant feeling, but compared to the way the rest of her body felt, it was a walk in the woods on a sunny day.

They turned another corner and at last entered the small four-bed emergency room.

"Here she is," the nurse announced.

The doctor came at once to her side, reaching over the gurney's railing and patting her hand. "We thought we'd lost you, Cheryl."

The comfort of his touch brought her to tears again. "I hurt . . ."

"I know you do, but not for much longer. This'll make it better."

She felt the sting of a needle and invited the wave of nothingness that swept over her. The last thing she saw before she slipped away was the clock.

Noon, she thought drowsily, and I'm on lunch duty.

Fifteen

A nurse slid back the sliding glass window that separated the waiting room from the emergency admissions desk.

"Mrs. Baker?"

Georgia looked up. "Yes?"

"The doctor wants to talk to you before you take Jill home. If you'd come with me?"

She stood, and spent a futile minute searching for but not finding her purse before remembering that she hadn't brought it. She crossed to the door which the nurse was patiently holding open for her.

Georgia followed her down a narrow hallway to a small office which was directly opposite the patient treatment area.

She hesitated. The curtains were pulled around all four beds and she didn't recall which was Jill's. They'd only let her see Jill for a few minutes and then had banished her to the waiting room so she wouldn't be in the way.

"May I see my daughter first?"

The nurse shook her head, indicating the door to the office. "The doctor's with her now. Why don't you have a seat?"

She sat obediently, although she'd been doing nothing but sitting since arriving at the hospital three and a half hours ago.

"Would you like coffee?"

"No, thank you."

The nurse smiled. "I'll tell him you're waiting," she said and left, pulling the door closed.

With nothing else to do, Georgia looked around. There was a standard-sized desk covered with journals, a shelf filled with medical reference texts, and about half a dozen styrofoam cups scattered here and there. A wire basket with the legend "Lab Tests" was nearly overflowing.

On the wall, a phone with its six lines lit up and blinking drew her attention.

She stared at it, noticing that the lights blinked in synchronization. That was why Dave hadn't returned her call after she'd left a message for him at the restaurant; he couldn't get through.

But he could have come, she thought. If he wasn't able to reach her by phone, he *should* have come. Jill was his daughter, too.

Georgia struggled against her growing sense of resentment at having to go through this alone, but the voice in her head refused to be silenced.

What kind of a father was he?

Where were his priorities?

And if he wasn't at the restaurant, where the hell was he? And with whom?

That was the question, the sixty-four thousand dollar question.

With whom?

Georgia got up from the chair, feeling peevish and slightly claustrophobic, but there wasn't enough room to pace and she couldn't exactly leave. She took a step closer to the desk and glanced at a yellow lab slip on top of the pile, thinking it might be Jill's.

It wasn't. Even if it had been, she wouldn't have been able to interpret it. She didn't know what an erythrocyte was.

She sat down again, feeling guilty for having looked. They were confidential records, after all. She'd invaded someone's privacy.

Why did nurses leave people alone in doctors' offices anyway?

Doctors' offices intimidated her, and had ever since she'd gone to her first fertility specialist ten years ago when she'd been unable to conceive.

Even the thought of those days was enough to make her palms sweat.

The door swung open just then and the doctor came in carrying a clipboard. "Hello."

She read the name off his hospital I.D. card. "Dr. Costa."

Costa was big, well over six feet tall, but he moved with a smaller man's grace. He sat on a corner of the desk, picked up the closest of the coffee cups, frowned into it and threw it in the trash. He seemed not to see the rest of the cups.

"Well, what can I tell you?"

"The nurse said I can take Jill home?"

He inclined his head in agreement. "As soon as she finishes her lunch."

"Lunch?"

"I wanted her to eat before I discharge her. Her blood sugar was on the low side."

"Is that why you've kept her so long?" When she'd first gotten to the ER, one of the nurses had told her that Jill was to be released within the hour. The hour had come and gone three times over.

"Yes and no," Dr. Costa said. "Tell me, how has she

107

been feeling lately?"

The question, although she should have expected it, caught her off-guard. A cold knot of dread formed in her stomach. "She hasn't been sick."

It wasn't much of an answer, but Dr. Costa seemed to accept it. "How about her appetite?"

"It's . . . she has a healthy appetite usually—"

"Usually?"

"Last night she hardly touched her dinner, but she didn't say anything about feeling ill."

"Hmm." He pursed his lips and tapped a pencil against them. "What about breakfast this morning? What did she eat?"

"Oh!" Georgia said, remembering the scrambled egg. "Yesterday she didn't eat breakfast either. I had to throw it out. And this morning she only had a bowl of cold cereal."

"Huh. But other than yesterday, you feel that she's been eating well?"

"Yes, overall. I mean, she's picky, but not any more than other kids her age."

"Picky. Well, maybe that's it."

"What?"

"Your daughter's blood tests show that she's borderline anemic. And since anemia is symptomatic of an underlying disorder, it's important to determine what physiologic mechanism is at work."

Georgia nodded to indicate she was following what he was saying.

"There are a number of etiologies, but I think hers is simple iron-deficiency anemia, which isn't uncommon in children. They're growing rapidly and many children won't eat the foods that'd give them what they need. Odd as it seems, children would rather eat dirt than red meat."

"The anemia made her faint?"

"Possibly, although I think it's more likely that she fainted from the low blood sugar and quite possibly shock. She did see her teacher get hit by a bus—"

"*Her* teacher? Miss Appleton?"

"That's right."

Georgia hadn't been told, and she felt bad for not having asked. "Was she hurt seriously?"

"She's stable."

Georgia knew equivocation when she heard it, and she realized she was prying. "I'm sorry," she said. "It's none of my business."

"You don't have to apologize."

"Yes I do. I looked at one of those—" she pointed to the basket of lab slips "—while I was waiting for you to come in."

Dr. Costa's smile warmed the room. "That's all right. Everybody does it. I do the same thing when I go to see my own doctor."

"Still—"

"Anyway, she's going to be fine."

Georgia wasn't sure who he was talking about, but she nodded and tried to smile.

He took a prescription pad out of the pocket of his lab coat, and in the process dislodged a stethoscope which he managed to catch before it hit the floor.

"I'm going to give you a prescription for an iron supplement for Jill," he said, not missing a beat, "and I want you to make sure she takes it. She'll need to be examined by your family doctor in about two weeks, to make sure we're on the right track here, that we're not missing anything."

"You mean, it could be something else? Other than her diet?"

"It could be."

She watched him as he wrote out the prescription. She kept silent until he'd finished and was tearing the sheet

109

off the pad. "Dr. Costa, what else could it be?"

He gave her a stern look. "I don't want you imagining the worst."

"I won't—"

"Mrs. Baker, I think both of you will do better if you're not worrying. Believe me."

What choice did she have?

Sixteen

"Are you finished?"

Jill nodded, putting the cover over the plate and pushing the bed table away. She'd been sitting cross-legged while she ate, and now stretched her legs out. "Can I go home?"

"As soon as you get dressed." The nurse pulled the panels of the yellow curtain together. "Do you need any help?"

"I've been dressing myself for a long time," Jill said archly.

"Of course." The nurse went to the counter where Jill's clothes were neatly folded and brought them to her. "Call me if you need anything."

Jill waited until the nurse had gone before reaching behind her neck to untie the hospital gown. She let it slip down her arms and shivered at the feel of cool air on her bare skin. Gooseflesh rose and she rubbed her arms, careful not to dislodge the small circular bandage in the crook of her right elbow.

They'd taken her blood.

She hadn't much liked that.

She touched the bandage gently and thought she could feel where the lab lady had stuck her with the needle. She bent her arm cautiously, imagining the blood spurting from the wound.

It had taken three tries to get the blood— "You have such tiny veins," the lady had said—and her arm was tender. Afterwards, the lady had volunteered to draw a happy face on the bandage and to "kiss and make it better," but she'd refused both offers.

Now she cradled her right elbow in her left hand and lifted her arm so that *she* could kiss the sore place. Her skin still smelled of the alcohol swab.

Jill wrinkled her nose.

Blood smelled better, she thought.

She pulled her blue sweater over her head and put her arms through the sleeves. She'd never noticed before how the sleeves bunched around her elbows, and she winced at the feel of the knit material pressing on her wound. She straightened her arm and readjusted the sleeve, but every time she bent her elbow, the sleeve accordianed.

After a moment's reflection, Jill pushed the offending sleeve up her arm, past the elbow.

"That's better."

She wriggled into her jeans and was reaching for her shoes when the curtain was drawn back again.

The doctor seemed to fill the cubicle.

"What's this?" He came to the bedside and ruffled her hair, not noticing when she smoothed it. "Need a hand, missy?"

"No." She tied the laces of her tennis shoe.

"At these prices, the least I can do is tie one of those for you." He took her stockinged foot and slipped it into the shoe. "Cinderella, I presume?"

Jill watched him draw the laces tight, make a lop-sided bow and tie it off.

"Your mother's signing you out." He winked at her. "It's a pretty ransom you've fetched, but then, you're a very pretty little girl."

As the doctor walked with her past the other beds, she saw Miss Appleton. Her teacher appeared to be asleep although the same lady who'd taken Jill's blood was now taking hers.

Jill slowed, watching with fascination as dark red blood welled into a large glass vial.

The doctor, his big hand on her back, ushered her along.

Jill glanced back over her shoulder, wanting to see, but one of the nurses approached and pulled the curtain back around the bed.

Seventeen

Before the nurse closed the curtain, Cheryl saw Jill Baker staring at her and felt a jolt of fear.

"Is anything wrong, dear?" the lab technician asked. "You've tensed up on me all of a sudden. Is something hurting you?"

Cheryl tried to take a breath so she could answer, but it was as though every muscle in her chest had tightened and now refused to move. The shot the doctor had given her had blunted the pain, thank God, but it hadn't made moving any easier.

"Now there's a foolish question," the technician went on. "All anyone has to do is look at you. Of course something's hurting, you poor thing."

Cheryl widened her eyes to show her alarm, but to no avail; the technician had turned her attention back to the drawing of blood.

"I'll be as gentle as I can. It'll just be a minute, so hold on for me."

"Jill," she whispered with great effort. It sounded slurred even to her. "She's here."

"What was that?"

"I think she asked for a pain pill." The nurse, who'd

115

gone directly to the head of the bed, stepped around to where she was in Cheryl's line of sight. "You shouldn't try to talk, honey. Just relax."

She tried again: "That . . . little girl."

"What did she say?"

"I'm not sure." The nurse turned away. "If I had that much Demerol in me, I'd be off in la-la-land."

"I know what you mean." The technician withdrew the needle from her arm, placed a cotton ball over the site and taped it. "There you go, bend your arm."

Cheryl tried to keep her arm straight so that the technician would realize she was resisting and make eye contact again, but she might as well have been a rag doll for all the control she had.

"Actually," the nurse said, "a margarita at lunch and I *am* in la-la-land. Ooh, a margarita! Doesn't that sound great?"

"I'm all for it." The technician had half-turned away and was sticking labels on the vials of blood. "You know any place that delivers?"

"I wish."

"Well that's it for me. I'm off." The technician picked up her blood collection tray and disappeared through the curtain.

The nurse continued whatever she was doing at the head of the bed.

Cheryl closed her eyes, exhausted.

A disembodied voice woke her by saying her name.

"Cheryl with a C, last name Appleton, spelled like it sounds."

There was a buzzing in her ears but she recognized the voice as Dr. Costa's. Through partially open eyelids, she looked for him, turning her head ever-so-slightly one way and then the other, but he was not in the cubicle.

"It was a bus versus pedestrian, and as usual the bus won. She has simple fractures of the lower left asternal ribs. We're going to tape her up."

Being taped didn't sound bad—it was certainly preferable to surgery—but whatever anyone said, there was nothing simple about her fractured ribs.

"Otherwise, she's got more than her share of abrasions, which were debrided in ER, contusions, and what is essentially a total body sprain. She's in a great deal of pain and can hardly move."

Perversely, Cheryl felt a sense of satisfaction at hearing the doctor confirm the legitimacy of her injuries. Her own family doctor had once suggested that she was a candidate for hypochondria.

No one could accuse her of that now.

"I don't have the heart to tell her she's going to feel worse tomorrow."

She didn't want to hear any more.

"Fine. I'll admit her to your service and tell the floor nurse that you'll be in to check on her this evening when you make rounds."

Dr. Costa came to her bedside some time later and she tried to tell him about Jill, to warn him about what the child had done and could do, but no matter how hard she tried to form the words, or how slowly she spoke, he misunderstood what she was saying, as the nurse and technician had. She finally gave up.

"We're going to give you another injection, a muscle relaxant this time, so we can tape up your ribcage without hurting you, and then the orderly will take you up to your room."

"Okay," she mumbled.

117

He gave her a peculiar look. "Boy, you've really got a case of mush mouth. I don't think I've ever seen anyone with a worse case. I wish I was a mind-reader."

So do I, she thought.

"Well, you'll be able to talk again soon."

All she could do was sigh.

Eighteen

"Thanks for coming to get us," Georgia said as she got into Faye's car after buckling Jill into the back seat. "I really appreciate it."

"Anything to help." Faye turned to look at her. "You weren't able to reach Dave?"

"No." Limiting her answer to a single syllable was the only way she was able to keep the grimness she felt out of her voice.

"No. Well, it's probably busy down there."

Georgia frowned, pretending to be occupied with her seatbelt.

"I'm sure he'll call you as soon as he can."

"Yes." She didn't mean to be unresponsive—Faye was a good friend—but her anger was too close to the surface to say more.

"Uh huh. Well then." Faye turned the key in the ignition and let the motor idle. "You want me to take you to the library so you can pick up your car or do you want to go home?"

The word had never sounded more welcoming. "Home," she said.

"Then home it is." Faye glanced in the rearview

mirror before backing out of the parking space.

They drove down the access road to where it turned onto Center Street. Waiting for a lull in the traffic, Faye drummed her fingers on the steering wheel. That and the blinking of the turn signal were the only sounds.

While they were waiting, a sports car made a left from Center into the hospital entrance and Georgia recognized the driver as the doctor who lived across the street. She could never remember his name, but this morning after Jill had gotten on the bus, she noticed him standing near his front window looking out on the street.

Now their eyes met, if only for a moment before he passed by, and she had a strong sense that he was somehow aware of what had happened . . .

She looked out the side window. The mirror was angled so that she could see Jill in the back seat, and she noticed that her daughter had closed her eyes.

Was she sleeping?

Drowsiness was one of the more frequent symptoms of anemia, she knew now. The nurse had given her a printed sheet with information on anemia, a frightening list of potential manifestations of the "condition" as the sheet referred to it.

The list included low grade fever, weakness, vertigo, headache, malaise, tachycardia, and palpitations, among others.

She thought back on the last few months, trying with hindsight to pinpoint the beginnings of her child's ailment, but there was nothing, no dramatic onset of frailty. And yet . . . how had she missed noticing how pale Jill had become? Pallor was also on the list.

Beside her, Faye cleared her throat. "Georgia?"

Reluctantly she looked away from the mirror. Faye's

expression was troubled, and she was staring fixedly at the road.

"Yes?"

"Listen, I've been . . . Do you want me to drive you to the restaurant? I can turn around . . ."

Georgia could not hold back a laugh, but she spoke quietly, not wanting to wake Jill. "That's the last place I want to go right now."

"Sometimes it's better to know."

"I don't want to know."

"Come on. Maybe what I told you yesterday, the things I said about Dave flirting with the new hostess, maybe I was wrong."

"Faye—"

"No, listen to me. Maybe he really *is* busy, or your message got misplaced, and it isn't at all what you're thinking."

"That's messages, plural, as in many messages, and I'm not *thinking* anything."

Faye winced. "Yes, you are. I can hear it in your voice, and see it in your eyes. I've seen that look before and I know the feeling. It's my fault that you're thinking what you're thinking. It's my responsibility to set the record straight."

"Please." Georgia rubbed at her temples which had begun to throb. "Can't we talk about something else?"

"All I'm trying to say is, he might be an innocent man. Right now, you're hurting because of suspicion, and there might not be a cause for it."

"What if there is?"

"Well—"

"If there is cause, if he is fooling around, I don't want to know right now. I don't think I can handle any more than this."

"You mean this thing with Jill."

121

"Yes."

"She isn't that sick, is she? I mean, they're letting you take her home."

Georgia thought for a moment before answering. "I don't know how sick she is. I didn't know she even was sick. If she hadn't fainted at school this morning, maybe I wouldn't know yet."

"I can see how that would worry you."

"It does." That wasn't the worst of it; try as she might, she hadn't been able to forget what the doctor had said: *Anemia is symptomatic of an underlying disorder.*

Disorder.

The word's vagueness scared her.

It could mean anything.

Faye pulled into the driveway and shut off the motor. "Let me help you carry her in."

"Thanks, Faye, but I can manage. You'd better get back to the library." With everything going on, work had entirely slipped her mind until this moment.

"Forget the library. I called for reinforcement hours ago." Faye hurried around the car. "I told them I'd get back when I got there."

Georgia gave her a hug. "You're a good friend."

"I'm going to try and be a better one."

Georgia retrieved the extra house key from underneath the mat, and between the two of them, they got Jill inside and put her to bed. Faye pulled the shades, shutting out the afternoon sun.

"Instant twilight," Faye whispered.

Georgia smiled and nodded, tucking her daughter in. She brushed the hair away from the sweet face and let her fingers rest on the child's brow.

If she had a fever, it was a low one. But then, it would be.

They left the door ajar so that if Jill called out, Georgia would hear her.

She led the way down the hall to the front room. "You want a cup of coffee?"

Faye shook her head. "I'd better be going. I know, I told them they'd see me when I got there, but tonight's the night for the Seniors Storytelling Hour. I don't want to miss out on that."

"Who could blame you? Listen, seriously . . . thanks for everything."

"I told you, anything I can do to help. Which reminds me, what are you going to do about your car? The damn things don't come when you whistle."

"I haven't even thought about it."

"Wait a minute!" Faye's eyes lit up. "I'll call the sheriff's office, and they can have an officer drive it home for you."

"Would they do that?"

"I don't know why not. There's not a lot going on in this town, the cops spend all their time eating donuts and drinking coffee. Sure they'll do it."

"If you think so . . ."

"Leave it to me. Where are the keys?"

"In my purse at the library."

"I'll send that with them, too. I'm sure we can trust them with your money."

"What money?" she asked, and laughed, this time genuinely. It was amazing how much better she felt, being home.

"That's the spirit," Faye said.

She followed Faye outside to the driveway. When they reached the car, Faye stopped and turned to face her.

123

"There's something I've been wanting to ask you," Faye said, and then hesitated.

"What?"

"How did you know?"

Georgia sighed. "You're not going to let it go, are you?"

"I'm not talking about Dave."

"Then what *are* you talking about?"

"Jill."

"I don't understand the question."

"This morning, when the sirens went off—no, it was even before that—you knew that something had happened to her. I'm asking, how did you know?"

Nineteen

"Noah, what a pleasant surprise," Alan Costa said when Huston walked into the emergency room. Costa was seated at a table with a stack of clipboards in front of him, filling out E.R. charts. "We weren't expecting to see you again for awhile."

"No?"

"Say, about three months." Costa regarded him with open curiosity. "Actually, it's gotten to where we set our calendar by you—"

Huston smiled; it was what Costa always said when they met. Small town humor, he supposed.

"—but usually you're here once and then only for a few hours. We know when you're coming and we're on our best behavior, but now you've gone and changed your routine, and caught us off guard."

"Things look about normal to me," Huston said, glancing around. Three of the gurneys were empty; on the fourth, an elderly woman in a lime-colored pantsuit was having her blood pressure taken.

"You should have been here earlier; the place was jumping."

Huston was thinking the same thing. "So I understand. They were talking about it in town—an out of control bus ran into some kids at the elementary school?—but the details I heard were a little sketchy."

"And more than a little wrong," Costa said, shaking his head. "First of all, it wasn't much of a bus, more like a glorified van someone at the school district painted yellow. It was only doing about ten miles per hour, if that. It wasn't out of control. And it was one of the teachers who got hit."

"Hmm. I thought small town gossip was more accurate than that."

Costa shrugged. "What we lack in accuracy, we make up for in volume."

"So what did happen?" Huston persisted. "Was the teacher badly hurt?"

"It could have been a lot worse. She was pretty banged up, naturally, and we had to admit her, but I think she'll be all right." He looked down at the paperwork spread out before him, selecting a clipboard from among the pile. "Speaking of which, I'd better finish her chart before her attending physician gets here."

Huston sat down opposite him. "So there weren't any kids injured?"

"Not by the bus." Costa paused. "You don't mind if I do this while we're talking? I hate to be impolite, but I get off at six and the nurses won't let me leave unless I finish with these."

"Go ahead. You were saying . . ."

"What was I saying? Oh yes, the official version of the accident is that the teacher was walking across the drive towards the school building, and for no apparent reason she just stepped in front of the bus."

"Ouch."

"No kidding. From what I gather, she was only struck a glancing blow, the kind you always see them walking away from in the movies, but in *real* life it was enough to propel her into one of the students, a little girl who was

126

standing nearby."

"Was the girl hurt?" He knew that Jill Baker was involved somehow, but he hadn't considered her to be one of the victims.

"She had the wind knocked out of her. She landed on her fanny and has a skinned tush to show for it, which may have hurt her dignity, but I think she was frightened more than anything else."

"You sent her home?"

"We did. A cute little thing, she was. Had a British accent, if you can imagine. Kept repeating that she had a sore bum. I told her to consider her injury as insurance against getting a spanking for the next few days. Now all her friends will be wanting the same thing to happen to them."

Huston laughed.

"Anyway," Costa said, "another of the students fainted at about that point, and the fire department medics brought all three of them in."

"What happened to the second child?"

"She's fine. Of course, if she'd hit her head on the pavement when she collapsed, it could have been a different story. But it turned out for the best."

"How so?"

"Well, I was concerned—fainting isn't common among children—so we ran a few tests on her and found she was anemic. If we hadn't done that, she might have gotten sicker."

Huston found it hard to keep from inquiring as to the patient's name, but he knew that as an infrequent visitor to the community—a stranger, really—it might seem odd that he'd ask.

"What's interesting to me," Costa continued, "is why anyone would step in front of a moving vehicle, no matter how big it was or how fast it was going."

"Suicidal," he said absently, distracted by thoughts of

the glimpse he'd gotten of Jill this morning as she'd waited for the bus.

"That's what the principal of Meadowbrook is claiming. He's been on the phone requesting we get a psychiatric evaluation on her."

"Oh?"

"As a matter of fact, I believe he's having the district send one of the school psychologists to interview her. I told him they could ask her anything they want, but not to expect her to answer."

"Why is that?"

"She's out of it." Costa signed the top chart with a flourish. "I doubt she could tell anyone her name, *if* she could talk."

"Dr. Costa?" A nurse had come up beside them. "Mrs. Lasalle is ready for you in bed one."

"Is she now? Okay." He stood and handed her the chart he'd just completed. "You want to send this up? They're waiting for it on Medical."

"Yes, doctor."

Costa started off and then turned back. "Oh . . . are you planning on hanging around for awhile, Noah?"

Huston nodded.

"Good. I want to talk to you about the association's profit sharing program."

"I'm looking forward to it," he said.

When Costa had disappeared behind curtain number one and the nurse returned to the nursing station, Huston reached and pulled several of the clipboards across the table.

Jill's chart was on top, and he scanned it quickly. It was incomplete—Costa apparently had been called away in midsentence and hadn't detailed the physical exam—but it was evident from the nurse's notes that Baker had been the child who'd fainted.

"LOC, cause TBD," the nurse had written on the line reserved for the nature of the complaint. Translated: loss of consciousness, cause to be determined.

A rather optimistic turn of phrase, he thought, since in many instances, even in these days of high-tech diagnostics, the cause often could not be determined at all.

It would be more honest to use a different acronym: WMGLAFO—we might get lucky and find out.

He extracted the lab reports from beneath the emergency room record and studied them. She had a marginally low hemoglobin, a borderline serum ferritin concentration—which meant that they couldn't rule out a disease process at work—and a low blood glucose level.

The question, of course, was what was causing the anemia. There were any number of possibilities, from the simple to the potentially fatal.

Huston couldn't help but wonder if doing what she'd been doing was taking something out of her.

Was she paying a price for the powers she had?

It was a provocative question, one he hadn't considered before in the five years he'd been watching her.

If she was hurting, would it stop her?

Wait a minute, he thought. It might mean nothing. The abnormal blood values could be entirely unrelated to the abilities that she had.

He had no proof that her physiology was different from any other child, regardless of the manner in which she'd been born.

Or to whom.

He closed those memories off and returned his attention to the chart.

There wasn't much more information to be had, but he noted with interest that her vital signs both on admission and discharge were within normal range. Her reflexes

129

were good, and, unlike her victims, there were no indications of slowed neurological response.

She hadn't even skinned a knee when she'd fallen.

Huston frowned.

He'd gotten what he'd come for, but he wasn't sure what to make of it.

Twenty

When it got to be five o'clock and Dave still hadn't called, Georgia went into the kitchen, closed the door, picked up the phone, dialed the restaurant's number, and hung up.

"Do it," she said to herself, her hand resting on the receiver.

She was as angry as she'd ever been, but part of her was also afraid. All it would take was a wrong word from him, or the wrong tone of voice, and she would cross that line beyond which she'd vowed she would never go.

The line existed, she knew, in all marriages, although not in the same form. Only by honoring its boundaries could a marriage survive. In her parents' case, the line was drawn at ever mentioning her mother's alcoholism or her father's pathological stinginess.

In her own marriage, the line prevented any suggestion that Dave hadn't wanted children, that it had been she and she alone who'd wanted a baby.

If she lost her temper and crossed the line, accusing him of being an indifferent father, of not caring enough about his daughter, he might say, "You're the one who insisted we adopt her. I was happy without kids."

131

He might remind her that she was the one who was unable to have a child. The physical defect was hers. He might say that if Jill was really his—if Georgia had borne him a child—he'd feel more for the girl.

If he said those things, the marriage would be over.

Georgia opened and closed her fingers around the receiver, undecided.

Could she talk to him calmly and stay within the limits of their understanding? If she heard the detachment in his voice, would she be able to ignore it?

Perhaps Faye had been right, and he was simply so busy he hadn't a chance to call—

"We've got a good crowd for lunch," he'd told her a few weeks ago, "from around eleven-thirty to two, but after that, you could fire a cannon through the place and not even raise dust. It's dead until five-thirty, or if we're lucky, five."

In the morning—she'd called for the first time before nine a.m.—she could understand that he was busy, dealing with vendors and all.

When the restaurant had first opened, she'd worked there about thirty hours a week in addition to her job at the library, so she knew.

There were hundreds of details involved in running a restaurant. He bought meat from one supplier, fruit and vegetables from another, breads and pastries from still another. He had to stock the bar, replenish the wine cellar, order cut flowers for the tables, make sure the linens were spotless and in adequate supply.

He had to worry about automatic dishwashers, walk-in freezers, the deep-fat fryer, and the massive ovens and stoves. The cash drawer on the register had been known to stick.

Then there were the annoying problems: chipped china, spotted glassware, and silverware that the dishwasher had failed to get clean.

The restaurant was still at the stage when its menu was being scrutinized, almost on a daily basis. There were recipes to try out and add, and slow-moving items to delete. When enough changes had been made, revised menus had to be printed, which invariably required working with a food photographer.

And then there was personnel. There were two shifts to cover, including an overlap during peak dinner hours. He had to interview and hire chefs, food prep workers, kitchen workers, waitresses, and, naturally, a hostess.

An attractive hostess, Dave had told her, could do a lot to bring in business.

Business must be booming, Georgia thought, the hours he'd been keeping lately. Just how damned attractive was this girl?

She hesitated a moment more, then lifted the phone and dialed.

"Baker's," a breathy female voice answered.

"David Baker, please?"

"May I say who's calling?"

That was a new twist; the calls used to be put directly through to Dave's office. "This is Mrs. Baker."

"One moment."

But instead of ringing through, she'd been put on hold. Bobby Goldsboro sang "Honey" in her ear.

She nearly hung up.

"I'm sorry, Mrs. Baker," the voice breathed, "he's not able to come to the phone just now."

"Oh?"

"If you'd like to leave a message, I'll be sure that he gets it."

I'll bet you will, she thought. "Yes, well. I called several times earlier. I don't think I spoke to you—I'm

133

sorry, I didn't catch your name?"

"Tanya."

"Of course, Tanya. Would you happen to know if he got my earlier messages?"

"No, I'm sorry, I don't," Tanya murmured. "Oh, excuse me—"

Georgia heard a rustling noise, as though Tanya had covered the phone with her hand. Tanya's throaty laugh was audible anyway.

"I'm glad you enjoyed your dinner," came the muffled purr. "Promise you'll be back to see me again soon? Maybe tomorrow?"

A male voice said something indistinguishable which elicited a delighted giggle.

Georgia looked heavenward. Give me strength, she thought. "Hello? Are you there?"

"Mrs. Baker? I'm sorry, but we're really busy—Friday night and all—but I'll tell Dave, I mean, Mr. Baker, that you called. Bye now."

The line clicked.

"By now," she echoed, and hung up the phone.

Jill had burrowed under the covers and was sound asleep when she went in to ask what she wanted for dinner, and she looked so warm and cozy, Georgia didn't have the heart to wake her.

She went into kitchen and stared into the refrigerator. There she found a single slice of American cheese—although the edges were beginning to dry out—and grilled herself a sandwich.

When Jill awoke she'd make a proper meal, but for now this would do.

She took her sandwich and a glass of milk into the front room and sat down. Eating standing up in the kitchen was something people who lived alone did.

There wasn't a lot to choose from on TV, but she turned it on and used the remote to tour the channels. She watched several minutes of a documentary on the plains of Africa, but switched the station when two lionesses brought down a deer by its neck.

It wasn't the violence that bothered her as much as the realization that in nature, it was often the female, the mother, who alone provided for the off-spring. The lioness had to be able to kill efficiently to feed her young. A female grizzly bear with cubs to protect was among the most dangerous animals on earth.

Not that it was all savagery. Care and nurturing were there, too.

By contrast, she had it easy, although sometimes it didn't feel that way.

She sighed and took a bite of her sandwich which had gotten cold. She tore it into halves and licked the butter off her fingers.

On the television, smooth-faced young men watched a sassy female bottom in cut-off jeans, all in the guise of advertising beer.

That was the real jungle.

She thought of Dave. And Tanya.

"Damn it." She didn't want to sit here feeling sorry for herself.

In the wild, females never fought over males; the male animal was good for breeding and little else.

Maybe they're the smart ones, she thought.

Don't expect more. Don't be disappointed. *Don't think about it*.

She dropped the sandwich on the plate. She'd managed to force down only about a third of it, but as it felt as though the cheese had become wedged in her windpipe. The milk did nothing to dislodge it.

Back in the kitchen, she looked for something to eat to clear the sandwich—a kind of edible Roto-rooter—and opened the vegetable crisper.

Celery and carrots.

Carrots?

"Hoppity!"

She'd all but forgotten about the rabbit.

Twenty-One

The sun had gone down, but the sky hadn't completely darkened, and she decided not to bother with the flashlight. It wouldn't be much help anyway; its batteries were nearly done for.

At first as she crossed the yard her brain couldn't make sense of what her eyes were seeing, but as she got closer to the rabbit hutch, there was no doubt.

Hoppity was dead.

Blood and bits of flesh still bearing fur were caught in the wire of the cage.

The body, or what was left of it, was suspended by one paw which had somehow caught in the upper right corner of the front of the cage. One eye was open and glassy, the other lost in the gore.

White bone showed. The skull?

Georgia stood at a distance of five feet of so, trying to think what could have done this.

"The dogs." She took a step closer and recoiled at the smell.

If it had been the dogs, though, why hadn't any damage been done to the cage?

Presumably, for the rabbit to have been killed while in its hutch, some weakness in the structure would have had to have been broached.

Two or three dogs leaping at the cage should have toppled it; it remained standing.

The teeth and claws of the dogs should have bent the wire, even broken through it in a few places; the wire was intact.

The soft ground around the cage, still damp from the rains, should show tracks of some kind; only one small human footprint was visible.

But if it hadn't been dogs, how had this happened? Who or what had done it?

Oddly, it looked almost as though the wire had been forced outward, as if the rabbit had hurled itself against the mesh.

Bracing herself, she moved closer. She could see that the body had stiffened.

Hoppity had been dead for some time now.

"Oh God," she whispered, and covered her mouth with her hand.

Whatever had done this might still be around, but Georgia didn't care.

She got a pair of gardening gloves and a shovel and dug poor Hoppity a grave. Taking a deep breath, she unlatched the door of the cage and reached in.

She could feel the coldness of the body even through the gloves, and that and the stiffness made her feel ill, but she worked at pulling the animal free from where it hung on its cage.

When she lifted it clear, a shredded bit of hide that had been pressed against the wire flopped onto the bare skin on her wrist above the glove.

She shuddered and brushed it aside.

After laying the rabbit in the shallow grave, she found that she couldn't just shovel the cold dirt on him. After a moment of thought, she went into the house and found a cardboard shoe box.

As small as the box was, there was plenty of room when she'd put the body in. She fit the lid on, placed the box in the hole in the ground, and resolutely began to cover it with dirt.

Not all of the dirt would fit, and she mounded the rest of it over the grave.

Her nose had begun to run and she realized that she was crying. She didn't have the strength to hold back her tears, so she lowered her head and let it come.

She wasn't sure how long she stood there, but when she went inside her fingers were too numb from the cold to properly grip the phone. She went to the sink and held her hands under the warm water.

If I could do that for my heart.

When feeling had returned, she went again to the phone and dialed the number from memory.

Twenty-Two

Beverly Wright crooked a finger and liberated a chocolate chip from the cookie dough, stuck it in her mouth, and then went into the front room to answer the telephone.

"Hello," she said, "I'm sorry, but I'm not able to come to the phone right now. But if you'll leave your name and number, and the time you called, I'll get right back to you. Please wait until you hear the beep and thank you for calling . . . *beep!*"

"Bev, it's Georgia—"

"Georgia, hi!"

"Are you there?"

"Sure. Couldn't you tell by the fake beep?"

"No, I—"

"No? I must be getting better at it. I hocked my answering machine a couple of weeks ago, but you're less than nobody in this town if you don't have one. I know people who have machines on their car phones, if you can believe it. Of course, a service is the best, but—hey, it's great to hear from you."

There was no answer for a moment, and then Georgia said, "It's been awhile."

"Hey, Sis, your voice sounds a little funny."

141

She perched on the back of the couch, and stuck her bare feet between the cushions to keep them warm. "Has something happened? Are you all right?"

"I'm not, actually. That's why I called."

"What is it? What happened?"

"A lot of things. . . ."

"Like what?" That bum, she thought, I'll bet the farm it's him.

"Well, Jill's sort of sick—"

"Sort of?"

"She's anemic. I found out today, after she fainted at school. The doctor doesn't know yet what's causing it, or at least he didn't tell me."

"Doctors," she spit out the word. "Ugh. What do *they* know?"

"Weren't you dating a doctor the last time we spoke?"

"My point exactly. Of course, he wasn't really a doctor; he played one on TV. The show lasted six weeks, and spent all of them in rating's hell. And deservedly so; it stunk. I think the producer's parking cars at Spago's. Anyway, he threw me over for a nurse, if you can believe it. A real one. Not that there was a lot that was real about her . . . Silicone City."

Beverly paused to give Georgia a chance to laugh, but there was only silence on her sister's end. Sometimes she tried too hard. "You still there?"

"Yes. I'm sorry, I'm not a good audience right now. I just don't think I can . . . I don't . . ."

"Hey!" She stood on the couch and began to pace its six foot length, the cushions supplying the bounce. "You really are upset."

"I am."

"It's more than Jill being sick, isn't it? There's something else?"

"Yes. It's complicated."

142

Beverly frowned and chewed at her lower lip. "I'm not real good at this, I know, but is there anything I can do to help?"

"I hate to ask . . ."

"You're not. I'm offering."

"Could you come up here?"

That gave her pause. "Up there? To Winslow, you mean?" Winslow, the middle of nowhere.

"Yes. I thought . . . I know you must be busy with your acting career—"

"It's not a career yet," Beverly said modestly, but she was pleased that her sister thought so.

"—but I was wondering if you and Katy might come up for a few days, or however long you want to stay. I'll make up the extra bedroom for you, and Katy can stay in Jill's room. I have to work, but in the evenings we can make popcorn and watch old movies and talk, and the kids can play . . . it'll be fun."

"Golly, Sis, it sounds great. I'd really love to, but I've got a call-back on Monday for a shot at three days on *General Hospital*. And three days at Guild rates is more than I make in a month at my temp job."

"How about the weekend then? You can come up in the morning and stay Saturday night. I've got Sunday off and we can have a picnic or something before you have to drive back."

"Well . . ."

"If you want, you can leave Katy here for Easter week, and I'll bring her to L.A. next Saturday."

"Leave Katy?"

"Sure. I know you say how much you like living in Hollywood, but after all that smog, the fresh country air will do Katy a world of good."

"Yeah, I can see what it's done for Jill," she said *sotto voce*.

143

"What?"

"Nothing. You know, I can't imagine not having Katy around for an entire week."

"It'd do her good to get out of the city," Georgia persisted.

"Maybe, but she kind of centers me, if you know what I mean. Having a kid at home keeps me from doing some of the crazy stuff people do in this town."

In fact, she'd often wondered which of them was the adult. Katy wasn't an average eight-year-old; Katy was special.

"Do you realize the girls haven't seen each other since they were babies?"

"Has it been that long?"

"It has. Why don't you ask her if she'd like to come and visit her cousin Jill?"

"Well, I would but she's not home."

"Not home? Where is she? It's . . . it's seven o'clock here."

Beverly smiled. "It's seven here, too. Believe it or not, and despite rumors to the contrary, Hollywood is *not* in another time zone. Another dimension . . . maybe."

"You let her go out by herself on a Friday night in Hollywood?"

"She's not by herself; she's at the Forum. The place is packed."

"Bev . . ."

"One of our neighbors had an extra ticket to a Lakers game and invited her to go along. She's a fan, she wouldn't dream of turning down a chance to see her team. Would you?"

"I might."

Beverly recognized that wry tone of voice and was glad to hear it. There was life in her older sister yet. Damn that Dave.

"Well . . . what about the week-end at least? You can

144

decide about the other later."

"Hmm. Let me think." She wound the phone cord around her index finger, the tip of which turned white as the blood flow slowed. Would that it were Dave Baker's neck, but then, his brain had to have been suffering from oxygen deprivation for years.

"Bev? Are you there?"

"Whoops! Sorry, I was gathering wool." She calculated her options: she had a dozen other things she should be doing tomorrow, including ten days' worth of laundry, but how often did her sister call her for help?

Never.

"Okay, sure," she said finally. "We can come up tomorrow."

There was no mistaking the relief in Georgia's voice. "That's great."

"Yeah, I think it will be."

"Make sure Katy brings a few changes of clothes, though, in case she decides she'd like to stay for the rest of the week."

"Will do. Listen, this call must be costing you a fortune . . ."

"That's something else I wanted to talk to you about. The will."

Beverly blinked. "What?"

"Dad's will."

"It's hardly a fortune," she said with as much disdain as she could muster when it came to money.

"Even so. I've come to a decision—"

"Georgia? Let's talk about it tomorrow, okay?"

"Okay."

"I'd better go. I'm in the middle of a batch of chocolate chip cookies. I'll bring you some."

"I'll supply the milk. And thanks, Bev."

*   *   *

145

When she'd finished baking the cookies, she stretched out on the couch and put an exercise tape in the VCR

There were few things more sinful than eating still-warm cookies and watching some aerobics princess sweating in her leotard.

Monday morning at the call-back, when she'd be the one sweating, was a long way away.

Twenty-Three

"Thanks, Roger," Katy Wright said as she started up the stairs to the second floor. She had on her tennis shoes but to be on the safe side, she tiptoed, holding onto the railing. "It was a great game."

"My pleasure. I'm glad your mother let you come at such short notice."

"Oh, she pretty much lets me do what I want."

"Really?"

"Amazing, huh. All that freedom and I haven't turned into a brat." She looked over her shoulder at him, watching as he trudged steadily upward. "So, are you going to ask my mom out?"

Roger's face reddened and he used a forefinger to push his glasses back to the bridge of his nose. "I don't think so."

"Why not? You like her, don't you?"

"Well, yes. Why wouldn't I?"

Katy couldn't think of a reason so she shrugged. "I don't know. Are you gay?"

"No, I'm not. Katy Wright, what kind of a question was that?"

"Just asking. My mom always says, you'll never know unless you ask." They'd reached the landing and she led the way down the hall to her front door. "You want to come in and say hi?"

He looked uncertain. "I don't know. It's late, almost midnight. Your mom might be asleep or . . ."

"In *déshabillé*."

Roger tilted her chin so that she was looking up at him. "How old are you, really?"

People were always asking her that.

"As old as I need to be." She dug into the pocket of her jean overalls and pulled out her apartment key. "So you don't want to come in?"

"I'd better not. It might embarrass your mom if I saw her, you know, in her bathrobe."

"Right." He'd be the one who was embarrassed; her mom didn't own a bathrobe. She unlocked both locks and turned the doorknob. "Anyhow, thanks for the game and the pizza afterwards."

"Katy?"

She raised her eyebrows expectantly.

"If I did ask your mother out sometime, do you think she'd say yes?"

"That's a very good question. What do you do for a living?"

"Katy, I'm serious."

"So am I. I can't answer your question until you answer mine."

He made a face. "You know very well I work in a bank downtown."

"Not a high-paying field unless you're in management," she observed.

"I work in New Accounts."

"Some potential for advancement, then. Steady work if the bank is solid. It's not one of those S & L's that wrote a lot of questionable loans and was left holding a ton of paper?"

Roger shook his head, apparently nonplussed.

148

"Hmm. A good job, a nice apartment, a nice car even if you do drive too slow. You pay your bills on time? What am I saying? . . . of course you do. You probably have an IRA and don't even wait until April 14th to fund it."

"Would you like to look at my income tax records? Or my checkbook?"

"That's all right," she waved it off. "*I* trust you. But after taking everything into account, would she go out with you? I'd have to say, probably not. I'm sorry."

"Why not?"

"You're a nice guy, Roger." She reached up to pat his shoulder. It was a stretch; he was also tall. "A very nice guy."

"Why do I have the feeling that I'm being insulted?"

"The thing about my mom is," she lowered her voice to a confidential level, "she craves excitement."

"I can be exciting."

"No offense, but I don't think so. You don't have it in you."

"We went out tonight, and you had a good time, didn't you? It was exciting."

"I'm a little girl," she said patiently, "it's not the same. And anyway, most of the excitement came from watching the game. You have to *participate* in a relationship, Roger, and nice guys just don't cut it."

"I don't see why not."

She counted them off on her fingers. "Nice guys show up when they're supposed to, call when they've promised to, don't lie or cheat or get phone calls from other women, and they always remember birthdays."

"So?"

"Where's the excitement in that?" She looked down the hall in both directions, to make sure no one was listening. "Some women aren't fully alive unless their blood is pumping with adrenaline and good righteous fury at the jerk who stood them up."

149

"You're telling me that she'd prefer me if I were a rat?"

"She's experienced with rats."

He gave her a skeptical look. "You're kidding me right?"

Her shoulders rose in an elaborate shrug. "Ask her and find out."

"Maybe I will."

She grinned and ducked inside the door. "Remember though, if she says yes, don't treat her too good."

The apartment smelled of slightly burnt something which a walk through the kitchen revealed to be cookies. Black-bottomed chocolate chip, her favorite.

Her mother had left the oven on and she turned it off. The sink was crammed with measuring cups and spoons, a couple of bowls and the dishes from breakfast.

She was really tired and she wanted to go to bed, but if there was an ant within a ten block radius, no doubt he'd find his way to their sink and the remnants of cookie dough. In the morning there would be a million of them, and her mother would go crazy with the Raid, and she'd wind up with a headache.

"Hopeless," she said. She took off her sweater and found an apron, not wanting to take any chances on splashing dishwater on her purple Lakers t-shirt.

When she'd finished in the kitchen, she discovered her mother asleep on the couch. The television flickering its blue light across her features, making her look exotic and mysterious.

If Roger saw her this way and wasn't already in love with her, he soon would be.

Katy sighed and went to get the comforter from her

mother's bed. When she flicked on the bedroom light she saw her own reflection in the mirror and wrinkled her nose.

No one had to tell Katy that she was plain. Brown eyes and brown hair, a dusting of freckles across her nose, and built sturdily, like a boy. Ordinary—from her pony-tailed head to her wide and not at all dainty feet.

Worse, she'd been cursed with a mother that men were crazy about. While no one would call her mother beautiful, she was easy to look at and had the kind of face that grew on you the more you saw it.

Interesting, distinctive, haunting.

Katy guessed she'd taken after her dad. Whoever he was, she thought, and turned off the light.

She covered her mother with the comforter, hit the off button on the TV, and went to bed.

Saturday

Twenty-Four

Dave Baker felt as though someone had put a steel band around his forehead and was tightening it just slowly enough to make him think it wouldn't get any worse. Not only had his headache worsened, it had lasted so long that he'd gotten to the point where he couldn't remember what it felt like not to have it.

Aspirin hadn't helped. Two codeine tablets hadn't helped, and may have even hurt. A desperation shot of whiskey, neat, had burned like fire going down but gave no relief.

"Eat something," one of the waitresses had suggested, but nothing—and he would never dare tell this to the chef—sounded appetizing.

In fact, the smell of food made his stomach queasy which made his head pound even more.

He'd closed himself up in his office, turned the air conditioner on full blast, lowered the lights, stretched out on the couch, and tried to wait it out.

At closing time he sent everyone home and locked up. It was his habit to stay and tally the day's receipts, and then prepare the deposit to take to the night deposit drawer at the bank, but he settled for putting the register drawer in the safe.

He'd count it later, when he *could* count.

The night air helped a little, and he drove with the window down.

There were pockets of fog along the way, and maybe it was the moisture in that which made the difference, but by the time he'd reached the neighborhood where he lived, he felt almost human again.

His headlights swept across the road as he turned onto his street, and he saw them standing there. His foot hit the brake and the Blazer hunkered down, the wide tires hugging the road as it came to a dead stop.

Dogs.

Their eyes had caught the light, glowing yellow as they looked in his direction.

Dave felt a flash of annoyance at the way they were just standing there, smack in the middle of the road, as if they had a right to be there, and *he* was intruding.

"Fucking dogs," he said.

There were four of them, or maybe five, it was hard to tell. The fog swirled around them, although driven by what he hadn't a clue; there wasn't any wind.

Even at a distance he knew these animals weren't your usual family pets out for a prowl. Two looked as if they might be a German Shepherd mix of some kind; another resembled a Doberman but had a squarer mouth.

The others—and there were three more, he could see now—were smaller, thin and hungry-looking, with quick eyes that he thought might glow on a moonless night.

They looked like wolves.

He reached down and found the handle to roll up his window.

If not for the lateness of the hour—it was past one— he'd lay on the horn and startle the shit out of them. He was tempted to do so anyway, but knew it wouldn't

156

endear him to the neighbors.

He took his foot off the brake and inched the Blazer forward, hoping that it might scare them off.

They stood there motionless.

Waiting, he thought, for him to make a move.

He envisioned himself flooring the accelerator and smashing into the center of the pack before they had time to scatter. Staring into those yellow eyes he could almost hear the solid *thump* as the bumper caught them and hurled them into the air.

Would they yelp? He hoped so.

His hands flexed and tightened around the steering wheel.

At that instant, as if by signal, they turned and fled into the dark.

It wasn't anything he'd done, he knew, but still he felt a moment of satisfaction.

As he pulled into his own driveway, he realized that his headache was gone.

Dave went into the kitchen, hit the lights, and headed straight for the refrigerator.

"Hallelujah," he said. "Orange juice."

Because there was no one to see him, he drank directly from the carton, pouring the tart liquid down his parched throat. He finished most of the quart before replacing the carton on the shelf and closing the door.

In recent months a red clip magnet on the refrigerator door had come to be the center of communication between Georgia and him. Usually he left notes for her, reminding her to do this or that, but tonight there was a folded note with his name on it.

Dave frowned, pulling it free.

Maybe she was peeved that he hadn't called her and this was her way of telling him to sleep on the couch.

Big deal, he thought. She ought to understand by now that when he was at the restaurant, he was at work. Just because he owned the place didn't mean he could waste time on personal phone calls.

None of his employees were allowed personal calls on company time. What was good for the goose, after all . . .

He opened the note and read:

Dave:

Beverly and Katy are coming tomorrow for a visit. Jill is not feeling well, so let her sleep in if she wants. Wake me when you get home. We need to talk.

Georgia

There were no other four words in the English language that he hated more than those: We need to talk.

He wadded the note into a ball and threw it in the trash before realizing that the smart thing to have done was leave the damned thing on the refrigerator. That way he could claim he'd never seen it.

He had no intention of waking his wife.

One headache per day was enough.

Twenty-Five

Mr. Rafferty had always been an early riser, for a long time by necessity and now by choice. It was quietest in that thirty minutes before the sun came up, and quiet was of value to a man his age.

He didn't look it, nor would he admit to it, because it was no one's business, but he was only a few weeks shy of his eighty-ninth birthday.

People took him to be seventy, maybe five years older than that, but no one guessed his true age, and he saw no reason to enlighten them.

He had no need for a hearing aid, but there were times he wished his hearing was less acute, because a hearing aid could be turned off. The noises that intruded on his private thoughts could not.

The country hadn't really been quiet since Ford had started the human race towards damnation by producing an American automobile. Should have left the noise and stink and bother of it to the Germans.

And airplanes; if he'd known that one day the sky would be swarming with those pesky little two-passenger planes, with engines that sounded like riled mosquitos, he'd have moved to Bora Bora and taken up basket weaving when he had had the chance.

There was altogether too much hustle and bustle going on, even in an out of the way place like Winslow.

So he got up, as he always had, at five-thirty, crushed a little eggshell into his coffee grounds and put the pot on the stove to perk, then sat by the kitchen window, savoring the solitude.

And the silence.

He especially enjoyed watching the sun come up. As many times as he'd seen it, nigh on eighty-nine years now, it still was something to marvel about.

Once he'd sat down with pencil and paper to add up how many sunsets he'd seen, and figured it to be over thirty thousand. That was a conservative estimate, he thought, subtracting maybe three or four years for his childhood when he was too small to be much help on the farm and was allowed to sleep to cock crow, and taking away a couple of years for those Sunday morning sunrises he'd missed as a grown man after a late night out on the town.

It'd been a goodly time since he'd been out on the town. If memory served, the last such occasion had been when he'd retired. His envious co-workers had poured so much booze into him that it nearly killed him.

Trying to save the company from having to pay his pension, he supposed.

Rafferty smiled remembering, but to be honest, he didn't miss the carousing. Never married, he'd been free to do as he pleased, but it took so much out of him . . . after he got to be forty or so, the night before was never worth the day after.

And even when he was a young buck and full of vinegar, those nights had never quite been the equal of daybreak. The women, they came and went, but the glory of a sunrise stayed with him.

Of course, his eyes weren't what they used to be and now he needed glasses to see it, but what the eye doctor

160

couldn't restore to him, his heart remembered.

When it was time to get about the day, Rafferty got up from his chair and went into the bedroom to exchange his slippers for a pair of worn loafers. He put on a second flannel long-sleeved shirt—he felt cold a lot of the time—and wrapped a long woolen scarf around his neck,

Now he was ready for his morning constitutional.

Almost ready, he corrected himself. Now where had he gone and left his cane?

A tour of the house failed to turn it up. After serious thought on the matter, he recalled that he'd left it in the cloak room at the hospital.

He preferred not to use it when he was working as a volunteer because too many of the patients commented on it when he escorted them to their rooms.

"Looks like *I* should be the one helping *you*," they'd say, and laugh at their witticism.

There were only so many times a person should have to hear the same stupid remark.

Well, he'd manage this morning without it.

He left the house by the back door, and when he turned from locking it, was stopped short by the sight of what appeared to be a dark mist rising from the Bakers' house.

A fire?

Rafferty sniffed the air, but did not detect any smoke. Whatever it was, it dissipated so quickly that he wondered if he'd even seen it.

He removed his glasses and wiped at his eyes which were stinging all of a sudden.

What was this? he wondered, a trifle uneasy. The stinging in his eyes grew worse. As he rubbed at them, knowing it was the wrong thing to do, he lost his grip on his glasses.

He held his breath, waiting for the sound of glass breaking, but luck was with him; they must have landed on the mat.

Rafferty reached blindly for the doorknob to steady himself while he leaned over to pick up his glasses, and rapped his knuckles sharply on the wood frame.

"Confound it." He'd driven a splinter into his little finger, sure as he was standing there. "If this doesn't beat all."

He brought the injured finger to his mouth and tasted blood. It was deep, then.

He reached for the doorknob again, more carefully this time, and righted himself, making sure his feet were planted firmly before bending down and sweeping the door mat with his fingers.

He felt the glasses and grabbed at them, but only managed to knock them off the side of the porch.

Rafferty straightened, disgusted with himself. He really was a doddering old fool.

Grumbling to himself, he dug out the key and, after a few tries, inserted it into the lock. Inside, he walked haltingly across the kitchen, arms in front of him so he wouldn't crash into anything, and to the junk drawer where he kept an extra pair of glasses.

He found them without any problem, and slipped them on with shaking hands. It was an old prescription, not as strong as he was used to, but they improved his vision to the point that he could see that the splinter had indeed drawn blood. It was too deep to pull out without a pair of tweezers.

First, though, he wanted to rescue his good pair of glasses.

He stomped down the porch stairs, his good mood

sorely tested by the last five minutes.

As he turned the corner at the bottom of the porch, the last of his serenity left him.

His glasses had landed in the gutted body cavity of a large black dog.

Flies buzzed above the carcass, and he thought he saw white-bodied maggots swarming inside it. He prodded the dog with the toe of his shoe.

The maggots worried him.

The dog hadn't been here yesterday, he was sure, but neither had it been dead that long—the flesh was still supple, he thought maybe he detected steam coming off the exposed innards as they cooled, and there wasn't much of an odor.

All of which supported it being a recent death, and yet . . .

Growing up on a farm, he'd seen his share of dead animals, and he knew that it took *time* before the maggots appeared.

Not a long time, but longer than this.

Flies had to find the body, and lay their eggs. The eggs took a while to hatch into grubs or maggots, the larval form of the adult fly. How many hours were involved, he wasn't sure—it wasn't the kind of information got passed on from father to son during polite conversation at the family dinner table—but it *had* to be at least a full day, didn't it?

And there were so many of them and they looked as if they'd been at it for some time.

Even so, this pooch had been alive an hour ago, he would swear it.

This was a fresh kill.

Rafferty studied the scene before him. After a moment he reached down and delicately plucked his good glasses from below the splayed ribcage.

One thing he knew, he didn't want to come face to face

with whatever had done this.

Around him the neighborhood was beginning to stir. The lay-a-beds reluctantly joining the day already in progress.

As he turned to go back in the house and call Animal Control to dispose of the body, he caught a glimpse of a face at a window. He waved.

It was the Baker girl, Jill.

Twenty-Six

Her mother was sitting quietly at the table, both hands wrapped around a coffee cup, and seemingly lost in thought when Jill entered the kitchen.

For a moment Jill hesitated, uncertain at the cause of the tension she felt in the room, but it did not appear to be directed at her, so she crossed to the table and sat opposite her mother.

"Good morning," she said.

Her mother glanced up, the frown on her face disappearing. "Jill, honey. I didn't expect to see you up so early this morning. How are you feeling?"

"Okay." In fact she felt very, very good.

"I'm glad." Her mother smiled and reached across the table, brushing the back of her hand gently across Jill's cheek. "You look well rested. Are you hungry?"

"A little."

"I only have a few minutes before I have to leave for work, but how about some hot cereal? With brown sugar and raisins? Would you like that?"

She liked hot cereal, so she nodded, and watched as her mother rose from the table and went over to the cupboard to get down a bowl.

"I'm going to make sure you eat right from now on,"

her mother said. She took a box of Instant Cream of Wheat from a shelf near the stove and studied the side panel. "The nurse at the hospital gave me a list of foods that are rich in iron and vitamin B."

Jill said nothing. She noticed a crumpled and stained piece of paper laying near her mother's coffee cup and tried to read it upside down. It was addressed to her dad, she saw.

"I mean, we can't have you fainting on the school playground because you're not eating sensibly," her mother was saying.

"No," Jill said absently. The note mentioned her Aunt Beverly and cousin Katy coming for a visit. When had this been arranged?

"Maybe some of the things that are good for you don't taste that great, but you can at least try them."

"Okay."

"I mean it, Jill."

"I know." It wasn't a matter of concern, really. There were other things to think about.

At the stove, her mother poured hot water into the bowl of cereal and stirred. "This looks pretty good—"

"Are we having company?" Jill asked, interrupting.

"What? Oh . . . yes. For the weekend at least, but maybe your cousin Katy can stay longer. You'd like that, wouldn't you?"

Jill considered it. "I don't know."

"Of course you would. You and Katy will be great friends—you're cousins, after all."

"I don't remember her."

"Well, you were still in diapers, so I don't suppose you would. We had an old-fashioned family get-together. Beverly and Katy, the three of us, Grandpa Wright, and, of course, your Grandmother and Grandfather Baker."

"We don't see *them* much anymore."

166

"No, no. Florida is a long way away, and they don't care to fly anymore, not that I blame them." Her mother sprinkled brown sugar onto the cereal and brought it to the table, placing it and a clean spoon in front of Jill. "I'll get the raisins."

The brown sugar had begun to dissolve and Jill quickly picked up the spoon to eat; she liked it best when the sugar still had a granular texture.

"That a girl," her mother said. She put a tiny lunch-size box of raisins near Jill's hand. "Eat up."

Jill ate.

Her mother remained by her side. "You scared me yesterday," she said.

All at once, her mother was kneeling beside her, brushing the hair away from her face and looking up into her eyes.

"I don't know what I'd do if anything ever happened to you. You're my baby, my precious baby. You're all that I have."

Jill saw tears form in the corners of her mother's eyes. Somewhere deep inside, she felt a pang of regret for the pain she would cause this woman. She knew very well that without her mother's intervention, she might have wound up like some of the others of her kind.

She touched her mother's face hesitantly. Offering comfort was not something she knew how to do, but the motions were simple enough . . . a touch, a smile.

Her mother's smile in return was dazzling.

"Look at me," her mother said, then turned Jill's hand over so that she could kiss the palm. "I've got to be at work in fifteen minutes and here I am crying."

"It will be all right," Jill said.

"I hope so, baby." She took a napkin from the holder and used it to dab under her eyes. "You be a good girl, okay? Make friends with Katy and I'll see you when I get

167

off work."

Jill inclined her head in agreement.

When her mother had gone, she sat for a time, drawing circles and shapes through the cereal with the spoon. She dumped the raisins on top and mixed them in, but although she liked the taste, she really didn't want to eat.

She was drawing nourishment from another source.

and disappeared into the blackness as she left the library, stopped to listen.

A twig snapped just behind her, and a hand reached out...

Twenty-Seven

Georgia reached the library a scant five minutes before opening, parking her car—which the police had indeed returned to her late last night—in its customary spot and hurrying across the lot.

"You didn't have to come in today," Faye said as she walked through the door.

"Oh yes, I did."

"Really, we could've managed without you. You know Saturdays are slow."

Georgia shook her head. "Think of my being here as crime prevention."

"What are you . . .? Oh, Dave."

"Dave," she agreed. She came around the counter and put her purse in a drawer beneath the microfiche reader. "Sometimes, I swear, I could strangle him, and with a smile on my face."

"What's he done now?"

"It's what he hasn't done. He never did call me yesterday, and I left him a note last night, asking him to wake me up when he got home. He didn't. I found the note in the trash this morning."

"Maybe he tried to wake you up but you were sleeping too soundly. When I'm real tired, a 747 could land on

169

my roof and I wouldn't hear it."

"Faye—"

"I know, make up my mind whose side I'm on. Well, I'm on yours, but I hate to see you upset like this. I'm not defending him, really; I'm trying to keep you from feeling so bad."

"For that, I thank you, but I think it's in my best interests if I stay upset."

Faye frowned. "This sounds serious."

"It is."

"Oh boy, What are you going to do?"

"I haven't decided yet." Georgia smiled and nodded at Mrs. Spencer, always the library's first patron of the day, and this morning two minutes early.

"You're not thinking the D word, are you?" Faye asked, her voice hushed.

It had occurred to her this morning when she'd gone into the kitchen, found the note missing from the refrigerator, and recovered it from the trash. She hadn't been able to rid her mind of the image of him tossing it in the garbage. If he had any regard for her at all, he wouldn't have done that. "Maybe."

There.

She'd said it, sort of.

"Oh Georgia," Faye breathed, her eyes widening. "I know how you must be feeling, but don't do it."

"Why not?"

"For a lot of reasons. How long have you been married? Ten years?"

"Thirteen," she said, and thought, *an unlucky number*. "What does that have to do with anything?"

"Thirteen years ago things were a lot different out there. Hell, even two years ago. But with all this disease and stuff going around, being single is not what it used to be."

170

Georgia shook her head. "I'm not interested in dating anyone—"

"*Now* you're not, maybe, because you're pissed at Dave, but in a year or so, you'll change your mind. It's a real hornet's nest out there."

"You're divorced. Are you saying that you've been celibate?"

"Well no, not *that,* but I'm very careful. But you, you're a romantic—the type who can be swept off her feet by a smoldering glance."

"Not anymore."

"I don't believe you—look at your taste in books— but even if it were true, you have to think about the financial consequences."

"I'm working," she said with a shrug.

"Right. So is Dave and you can't pay your bills on both of your salaries. How are you going to survive on your paycheck alone?"

"I could cut back on a lot of things."

"Like what? What wild extravagences have you been indulging in that I don't know about? What luxuries can you dispense with?"

Georgia couldn't think of any. "Well . . ."

"That's what I thought. You make, what? Thirty-five percent of your joint income?"

"A little more."

"Call it forty. If you divide your bills fifty-fifty, can you pay your share and make it on what's left? Will you be able to cover the rent, utilities, groceries, insurance, clothes, and transportation?"

"There's always child support—"

"I've never met a woman who was able to support her child on what her ex-husband gave her alone. It's a pittance. And the checks are late half the time, or they bounce, or don't come at all."

"I do have an inheritance coming to me," she said. "The money my father left me."

"You'll have to split that with Dave, too. California is a community property state."

"It doesn't matter. I'd manage."

"Uh huh." It was Faye's turn to smile at Mrs. Spencer who was browsing in the new book section a few feet away. "What happens is, you won't be able to afford the house payments on your own, so you'll have to sell it and split the profit if there is any, which there might not be. Winslow isn't a hot market. Then you rent an apartment for you and Jill, some little hovel, with hot and cold running water leaks."

"When we were first married, we had a studio apartment, so small that we—"

"—had to take turns turning around," Georgia finished for her. "And you were happy. Sure, you can do it, scrape out a living, but why should you when he's living high on the hog?"

"He wouldn't be, would he?"

"He would after he moves in with someone like that hostess."

"Tanya."

"Her name is Tanya? What, did her mother wake up in the hospital the morning she was born and say, '"Hey, I'd like my daughter to grow up to be a bimbo. Now what's a good name?"'"

Georgia laughed. "Honestly, Faye."

"Never mind. Anyway, Dave finds an adoring woman, or slut as the case may be, who takes him to heal the wounds inflicted by his bitchy ex-wife who's sucking the very blood out of his veins. That's you."

"So I gathered."

"Anyway, he's doing well, spending afternoons by the pool, and evenings in the hot tub. Maybe fitting in a game

172

of tennis. Tanya feels so sorry for him, she doesn't even ask him to pay a share of the rent—"

"Wait a minute," she held up her hand. "How much money does *she* make?"

"More than you do."

"I find that hard to believe."

"Well, believe it or not, it's true. Bimbos are never poor. Don't ask me why, I don't know. Nobody knows; it's a quirk in the economic system. Maybe they save a lot by not buying underwear, or maybe they've got a good union. The point is, he's doing better than he's ever done in his life, and you're doing worse."

"It sounds gruesome—"

"That's the point," Faye said, tapping her finger on the counter for emphasis.

"But how about the way I feel?"

"Okay, right now you're steamed. I would be too, but really, what happened? You had a scare, but it turned out that Jill will be fine, and there was nothing he could have done anyway."

"He could have been there for me."

"Your vows said 'For better or worse, in sickness or in health, and in case of an emergency, be there to hold my hand?'"

"It's the principle that matters. And you left out the part about forsaking all others."

"Honey, you don't get a divorce over principles. As for forsaking all others, if you come home and there's a naked woman wallowing in lime jello in your bathtub, *then* you get a divorce."

Off to their left, Mrs. Spencer snorted and covered her mouth with her hand. Throwing them a guilty look, she sidled off into the stacks.

"All I'm saying is, think about it. Remember that divorced women raising children alone make up most of

173

the households living below the poverty line. Don't do something in the heat of the moment that you'll live to regret."

Georgia sighed. "I won't."

But neither, she thought, am I going to lay down and let him walk all over me.

Twenty-Eight

"Well, here we are," Beverly Wright said, pulling in beside a Chevrolet Blazer in her sister's driveway. She revved her engine twice before switching it off. "What do you think, kid?"

Katy made a face. "Now I know how Lewis and Clark must have felt."

"Come on, it's not that bad." She released her seat belt and reached into the back seat to rummage for her overnight bag.

"It's in the middle of nowhere."

Beverly couldn't argue that. "But look at how blue the sky is."

"It's nice. How much time per day do you think a person spends admiring the sky?"

"There are other things to do." She opened the car door and got out, then waited patiently for her daughter to do the same. "Watching the grass grow, for example. Or if you're lucky, watching paint dry."

Katy's expression indicated she believed it.

"Don't forget you'll have your cousin Jill to keep you company; I'm sure you two will find all kinds of things to do."

"I can hardly wait."

Beverly draped an affectionate arm around her child's shoulder as they started up the walk. "Try not to be a sour puss."

"I had plans for today," Katy said. "I have a life, you know."

"Rank has its privileges, you know. And when you grow up and you're the mother—"

"*I'm* not having kids."

"—then you can be the privileged one who decides what you want to do every weekend and know the joy of listening to your sniveling brats complain."

"I don't snivel."

"Oh? What was that trophy on your dresser for? I thought it was for sniveling," she teased. "Sniveler of the Year?"

That brought a hint of a smile. "It was not."

Beverly leaned down and kissed Katy on the ear. "You can be a pain sometimes."

"Mom, I live for these tender moments."

She laughed. "So do I."

Dave was about as good-looking as she'd remembered him being, which was very, but also just as cold. There was a kind of nothingness in her brother-in-law's eyes that reminded her of a particular fish in the aquarium at her dentist's office.

She went to her dental appointments hoping against hope that one day she would see that fish floating belly up.

She felt much the same about Dave.

"Beverly," he said, and extended a hand to her. "How are you? And how are things in Hollywood?"

"Keen, absolutely keen."

"And this is Katy?"

"Actually," Katy said wonderingly, as though the

176

hought had never before occurred to her, "I am."

"Well, Katy, I think Jill's in her room, if you want to come and say hello." Belatedly, he seemed to notice that hey had luggage, and he took both cases before starting down the hall.

The pictures that Georgia had sent her of Jill didn't do he child justice. Her niece looked up as they stood in the doorway, and Beverly was stunned to the point of being nearly speechless.

In her business, she'd come across some pretty kids, but this one was achingly beautiful.

"Jill, this is your Aunt Beverly and your cousin Katy," Dave said.

"Hello," the girl said.

Katy crossed to where Jill was sitting and promptly plopped down beside her. "Hi."

Feeling wretchedly traitorous, Beverly couldn't help but see the contrast between the two of them, one plain, the other breathtaking.

"Well, you've certainly grown since the last time I saw you," she said, finding her voice. She glanced at Dave who appeared immune to his daughter's looks, and she wondered at that.

"What've you got?" Katy asked.

Beverly hadn't noticed before, but she saw now that Jill had a wooden-lidded box in her lap, and she had covered it with both hands.

"Nothing. My collection."

"Can I see?"

Jill tilted her head slightly, her gray-green eyes looking, Beverly realized, at she and Dave. "Private, huh? That's okay, we understand, don't we, Dave?"

His smile was fleeting. "Sure. Listen, I hate to run off like this, but I've got to get down to the restaurant. Do you mind if I show you to your room?"

"That's fine." She winked at Katy. "Be good or I'll sell you to the gypsies."

"Promises, promises," Katy said.

The extra bedroom was surprisingly secluded, at the very end of the hall. Better yet, it was spacious and had its own bathroom.

"I think this was a great idea," she said to the room after Dave had left.

Katy might be unappreciative, but she was glad to get out of the city once in awhile. There was no place like LA—and she loved it—but there were times when the relentless pace of it was overpowering.

She sat on the bed and bounced lightly, testing the mattress, then kicked off her shoes and scooted over until she was in the center. The middle of her own bed sagged, and she'd learned to sleep on the firmer sides, one hand curled around the bedpost to keep her from falling back.

"Heavenly," she murmured, and pulled the bedspread around her. Her eyes closed of their own volition. She hadn't felt particularly sleepy until just this minute, but now . . .

There was a knock on the door.

She groaned. She sincerely believed that kids were equipped with some kind of radar which told them when their parents were trying to sleep. "Yes?"

"Mom?"

"Yes."

The door opened and she sensed rather than heard Katy come to the side of the bed. Her eyes didn't want to open, and she wasn't inclined to force them to.

"Is it all right if Jill and I go and get an ice cream cone?"

178

"If you want."

"Can I have some money?"

"It's in my purse. Get it yourself, baby."

"Thanks."

She heard her purse being unzipped and then a general jingling as her daughter pawed through it.

"Enough for a banana split instead?"

"If I've got it."

"You do."

Beverly heard a thump as Katy dropped the purse back to the floor and then the bed dipped as her daughter climbed up and kissed her on the cheek.

She smiled, her eyes still closed. "That was nice."

"There's more where that came from," Katy said, and then she was gone.

Beverly drifted toward sleep.

I should have told her to be careful, she thought drowsily, and smiled at the absurdity of it.

Every day Katy braved the streets of LA, and she'd never had a problem she couldn't handle. If the kid could survive that craziness, what was there to worry about in a small town like this?

Twenty-Nine

Katy felt as she imagined an anthropologist must when faced with a heretofore unimagined civilization, amazed and slightly dumbfounded. All she needed, she thought, was a pith helmet and maybe a whip.

Indiana Jones and the Temple of . . . what?

Her mother had called the town "quaint" when they'd driven through, marveling at the hand-carved wooden street signs and Colonial-style storefronts.

It was even more quaint on foot.

Main Street was a two-lane road. She didn't see a single fast food restaurant, video rental store, photocopy center, frozen yogurt stand, sushi bar, or discount clothing outlet. Nor were there any businesses with names she recognized.

Katy supposed this far out, they'd never heard of chain stores or franchises.

No Winchell's, Radio Shack, Kragen's Auto Parts, Crown Books, Federated, or Thrifty's.

More significantly, under the circumstances, was the fact that there wasn't a Baskin-Robbins, Swensen's, or Haagen Dazs ice cream parlor in sight.

The ice cream store they were going to was called Thelma's. She'd bet next week's allowance that there

181

hadn't been a marketing survey done on *that* name.

"Do you have a movie theater?" she asked Jill as they walked. Theaters were, to her way of thinking, the basic foundation of civilized life.

Jill shook her head. "There's one down in Leland."

"How many screens?"

That earned her an odd look. "Just one."

"Oh. Has it got Dolby?"

"I don't know what that is."

"It's a movie sound process," Katy explained. "Like stereo, only better. A good system can shake you right out of your seat."

"Well, we don't go to the movies very often."

"I guess not." She noticed their reflection in one of the store windows and found her eyes drawn to the image of her cousin's face. Jill, she saw, was watching her. "What *do* you do around here?"

"Go to school. Watch TV. Collect buttons."

"Uh huh." Jill had shown her the collection after the grown-ups had left, and while all the different colors were kind of pretty and it was sort of fun to sift them through your fingers, it hardly seemed to be something a kid would do for fun. "Is that all?"

"I guess so."

"What about playing with the other kids? You aren't the only kid in town, are you?"

"No, but I don't play with the others."

"Why not?" She bent down to pick up a rock which lay in the middle of the sidewalk, hefted it and then put it in the pocket of her overalls.

"I don't like them."

Katy frowned, "None of them?"

"No."

"You mean, you don't have one friend?"

Jill shook her head.

"Wow," she said, and fell silent. She wondered how

much that had to do with Jill being so pretty.

At her own school, the prettier girls tended to keep to themselves, preferring each other's company. As if, she often thought, they were worried that being ugly was somehow catching, like the measles.

Her mom had once dated a guy who claimed their existed an ugly stick which had the power to change a person's appearance.

"Looks like she got hit with the ugly stick," he'd say about someone he saw passing on the street, and then laugh.

Katy, at age four, had believed him, and she'd gone to her mother in tears. "Someone hit me, mama, with that ugly stick."

"There's no such thing," her mother told her. "Damn it, Bobby, what lies have you been filling this child's head with?"

Bobby had moved on shortly after that.

Still, as they said in Hollywood, it was an intriguing concept.

If such a thing did exist, there were a few girls she knew that she'd enjoy using it on. *Then* see who they ate lunch with.

Not Jill, though.

Her cousin was a bit standoffish, but Katy could tell it wasn't out of conceit. Jill probably knew she was pretty—how could she not?—and yet Katy had the impression that her looks weren't important to her.

Better than that, when Jill looked at her, Katy didn't feel that she was being judged and found wanting. What she saw in her cousin's eyes was mild curiosity, and none of the smug superiority that might have been there.

She decided she liked Jill even though they weren't true blood relatives.

"My mother says I can stay longer than the weekend if I want to," Katy said.

"Do you think you will?"

"It depends. I mean, I'm used to staying pretty busy. I like to do stuff."

"What stuff?"

"Lots of things. Movies, video games, sports, hanging out, that kind of thing. And when we can afford it, there are all those tourist things. Disneyland."

"I've never been."

"You'd like it," Katy said. "They've got these lands, Fantasy Land, and Tomorrow Land, and there's Bear Country, and the haunted house, a jungle cruise, and all kinds of stuff. Space Mountain is my favorite, the ride is so fast. You *have* to see it, it's the best."

"It sounds . . . interesting."

"Bug your parents until they take you," she advised.

"I don't think they would."

"Why not?"

"My father's too busy."

"Then ask your mom. My mom and I go lots of places, just the two of us. We came up here, didn't we?"

"There isn't time," Jill said.

Katy didn't know what to make of that, but hadn't a chance to ponder it; they'd arrived at the ice cream store.

"Thelma's," she said with a shake of her head, and they went inside.

Thirty

The first thing Katy noticed was that this place didn't have glass counters. You couldn't see the ice cream, or watch as the guy served it up.

She guessed people in small towns were more trusting that those in the city, but personally she wanted to see that the ice cream scooper was clean when it dipped into her flavor.

She closed her hand around the five dollar bill in her pocket next to the rock. "You can have whatever you want," she said, pleased to be able to share the wealth. "It's my treat."

Jill smiled faintly.

There was only one customer other than themselves, an elderly woman who was having some difficulty making up her mind from among Thelma's twenty or so choices, and as they waited their turn, Katy took the opportunity to study her surroundings.

The shop had wood-paneled walls, and featured booths rather than those annoying wobbly-legged white metal tables so prevalent in LA's ice cream parlors. The cushions in the booths were upholstered in a dark, rich red fabric. The floor was a black and white checkerboard pattern, and spotlessly clean.

Overall, the effect was understated, but elegant.

Katy approved; she secretly suspected that the bright colors favored by some food joints were intended to assault the eye and blunt the senses, and thus dull the tastebuds to their mediocre fare.

By contrast, good old Thelma's was restful. Even the tinkle of the bell which rang when they'd opened the door had sounded muted.

"Next," the counterboy said.

They stepped up to the counter as the old lady turned away. After all the indecision, Katy noted that she'd picked strawberry.

"I'd like a chocolate ice cream soda, with three scoops, please," Jill said.

The boy, who might have been sixteen, gave her cousin what Katy could only call a hot look. She feared for the ice cream's safety.

"Whatever you want, pretty baby," he said, and grinned. The tone of his voice was equally as heated as his eyes had been.

Katy raised her eyebrows. His suggestiveness was the kind of thing she often heard in the city, usually from unshaven old men who called out from dark doorways in abandoned buildings as little girls passed by. She hadn't expected to hear it here.

"Hey," she said, "the ice cream is melting. You want to knock off the heavy breathing?"

He looked surprised, and a tinge of pink appeared on his acned cheeks. His eyes darted from her to Jill and back again.

"Just being friendly," he stammered.

"Save it." She brought out the five dollar bill and showed it to him. "This is money. We came in here for ice cream, and nothing more. My cousin wants an ice cream soda and I want a banana split, extra whipped cream, and hold the nuts."

"Okay, okay."

She paid for their order, pocketed the change, then took Jill's hand and led her over to one of the booths. "Do you know that guy?"

Jill glanced toward the counterboy, as if only now noticing him. "He's Kevin's older brother. One of the boys in my class."

"Well, he's a creep."

Jill inclined her head in what Katy took to be agreement but didn't comment.

"A regular dirty old man in training," she said with distaste, watching him across the room. She would have to inspect her banana split carefully before eating it; she wouldn't put it past him to spit in it or do something else equally disgusting.

"I wouldn't worry about him," Jill said. She depressed the lever on a straw dispenser, and delicately extracted the straw from the slot.

The guy brought their order to the table, put the glass boat in front of Katy and held the soda for a second before handing it to Jill.

"Enjoy it," he said.

It seemed for a moment that he might just stand there and watch them eat, but thankfully the bell rang as the door opened and another customer came in. With obvious reluctance, he returned to work.

"His parents ought to get him fixed," Katy said when he was gone. She frowned and turned the banana boat to check the other side. It looked okay to eat, so she picked up her spoon.

"What do you mean, fixed?"

"You know, like they do to dogs." Didn't she know *any*thing? "They fix them so they can't breed. It calms them down."

187

"Oh."

Katy took a bite of her banana split, savoring the blend of flavors. "This Thelma makes good ice cream, I'll give her that."

"He only put two scoops in my soda," Jill said. "I asked for three."

They both glanced toward the counter where the lady was counting coins into his outstretched hand.

"Forget it," Katy advised. "If you go up there, he's just gonna say something nasty. Take my word for it, it's not worth it."

"I wanted three scoops."

These young kids, she thought, glad she was eight and not seven anymore.

"You can have some of mine. Look, I can scrape the butterscotch topping off the vanilla, and—"

"I asked," Jill said again. Her hands had closed into fists. "I even said please."

Katy was about to say that people didn't always get what they asked for when the counterboy screamed. The sound sent shivers down her spine.

"Oh my God!" the woman customer said, her face turning ashen. "Oh my Lord."

Katy jumped up and ran to the counter, leaning across and looking at the boy who was on his knees on the floor with his back to her.

"What happened?"

The lady didn't answer. Instead she hurried to the end of the counter where it opened into the shop and went straight to the phone on the wall.

The counterboy's shoulders were shaking, and he seemed to be sobbing. "My hand," he cried between gulps of air, "my hand."

"What happened?" Katy repeated, this time louder.

The woman pointed towards a huge mixer with a glass container which sat on a workshelf opposite the ice

188

cream bins. Katy stared at it, not understanding. What did making a strawberry milkshake have to to with this guy crying on the floor?

But then she saw that the color of the shake was wrong, it was way too dark. Strawberries never got *that* red. Those were swirls of blood amidst the vanilla.

"He put his hand in there," the woman said finally, but it was more to herself than to Katy. "He put his hand in and hit the switch, as pretty as you please."

Fascinated, Katy noticed thick drops of blood on the checkerboard floor. It looked nothing like movie blood, she thought.

There was nothing pretty about it.

She turned, expecting to find Jill beside her, but her cousin had remained at the table, and was sitting there calmly drinking her soda.

Thirty-One

Noah Huston heard the siren well before he saw the flashing lights. He slowed his car and pulled to the side of the road to allow the ambulance to pass. As it did he caught a glimpse of the patient, a male who looked to be in his teens.

The young man's face seemed familiar, but he couldn't place it.

He accelerated back into traffic, which was light as always. Two hundred yards and three cars ahead of him, the ambulance slowed to make the left turn onto the hospital grounds. As was the custom, the driver killed the siren once they were off the public road, and it died out with a low-pitched growl.

He drove past the hospital, casting a sideways glance at the emergency room ambulance bay where the patient would be unloaded. Already a nurse was standing by.

These people dispensed good medicine; no one could accuse them of the indifference which seemed to plague the city hospitals where he worked.

Even he'd begun to feel it, a curious deadening of emotional response to the people who brought their shattered lives to him for healing. Once it had excited him, to think that he could intervene in a crisis and by his skill, change its outcome.

How long had it been since he'd felt that way?

Too damned long.

Idealism hadn't a prayer when faced with realism, and in the real world, patients died even if you did everything right. Maybe they were tired of living, or maybe people came with an expiration date that no one could see except for a higher power who in the interest of quality control took the product off the shelf.

"Boy, are you losing it," he said to his eyes in the rearview mirror. "God as a grocery clerk."

His hatred of death was the legacy of his days and nights as a resident, when as the low man on the totem pole, he'd been the one who had to "pronounce" the patients who died during his thirty-six hour shift.

It was the height of medical arrogance, he'd always thought, that a patient could be blue-faced, cold, and as stiff as a board—some of them actually had been—but they weren't officially dead until he, the mighty doctor, pronounced them so.

Once upon a time, during a particularly trying and tumultuous shift, he'd been tempted to refuse to pronounce a patient, just to see what the ramifications might be. Would they continue giving meds? Bring a breakfast tray? Take vital signs?

Why not? he'd thought with the crystalline logic of a young doctor who'd had two hours of sleep in a day and a half. They could continue to bill the insurance, couldn't they?

In the end, however, he'd gone into the room, pulled back the sheet, placed the stethoscope on a motionless chest and verified that the patient was indeed dead. He signed the chart and then went and stood in the stairwell, shaking with exhaustion and rage that he couldn't save everyone's life.

But that was long ago, before any of this started.

Before he would come to realize that he might have to take a life to save many.

He had to correct the mistake he'd made by cutting that cord.

Huston parked on the street and checked the address he'd written in his notebook.

The number that he was looking for turned out to be a neat wood-frame house to the left of where he'd parked. He crossed the road and started up the pathway.

Voices were coming from the opened front door, and when he reached the doorstep he was nearly bowled over by a herd of red-haired children who quickly disappeared down the street.

"Don't be ruining your appetite for dinner now," a woman called after them, "or you'll be having liver and onions for breakfast, and *I mean it*."

"Mrs. Lassiter?"

The woman appeared in the doorway, as red-haired as her brood and easily six months pregnant. "I am. You're the doctor who called?"

"Yes," he held out his hand. "Noah Huston. I hope I'm not interrupting." He hadn't realized it was near the dinner hour, and he glanced at his watch. It was after five.

"Not at all. Come in."

He followed her into the living room and watched as she lowered herself awkwardly onto the couch.

Catching him watching, she smiled. "This is the easy part. It's not long and I'll be needing a crane to help me get up from here."

"When are you due?" he asked, more from habit than anything else.

"There are two schools of thought on that," she said. Her right hand stroked her belly affectionately. "My doctor thinks mid-June but I'll be damned if I'll have a baby right when the others are getting out of school. I'm shooting for Memorial Day."

He nodded as if he understood, then cleared his throat. "Mrs. Lassiter, I wanted to talk to you about Sarah. About what happened yesterday at school."

"That was a terrible thing, wasn't it? Poor Miss Appleton—"

"Yes, but—"

"—and I tried to stop by and see her today when I went in for the ultrasound, but there was a psychologist with her and I didn't have time to wait. Can you imagine, they think she did it on purpose?"

"About Sarah?" Huston prompted gently.

"I'm sorry, but it's insane for them to suggest that she's, well, insane. We've only lived here since January, and I'm not saying I know her that well, but Miss Appleton was wonderful to Sarah, very attentive."

"That's nice, but—"

"It's difficult on children to have to change schools in mid-term and she went out of her way to make Sarah feel at home. Why, she was the one who suggested we wait and have Sarah's party during Easter week so more of the kids could come."

"Mrs. Lassiter, excuse me for changing the subject, but about Sarah . . . ."

"What about her?"

"Has she told you about yesterday?"

"Hardly a word. But then—" she smiled broadly "—with the other five as competition, sometimes she can't get a word in edgewise."

He nodded slightly. "Do you think she would have told you if something . . . strange . . . had happened?"

"Stranger than being knocked down by a flying teacher?" she said, and laughed. "I'm sorry, doctor, but

194

it is absurd when you think of it."

"Yes, it is. And that's why I'm here. I need to find out if she noticed anything unusual prior to or after the accident."

"Well, I suppose you're going to have to ask her."

"Will she be back soon?"

"I don't imagine they'll be too long. They've gone off to the market for eggs. We colored a whole dozen before one of the boys pointed out that we hadn't bothered to hard-boil the blasted things."

"Would you mind if I waited?"

"Not at all, if you don't mind if I leave you to yourself while I finish a few things in the kitchen."

"That's fine. Oh, one other question?"

"Yes?"

"I understand that Sarah is British . . ."

"Oh, that," she said. "Yesterday she was British, today she's French, and tomorrow she'll be, I don't know, Chinese or something. It's her way of being different in a family of carrot-tops where the first thing people notice about us is this." She fingered a lock of her hair.

"She had the emergency room doctor fooled," Huston said.

"Sarah's a natural-born mimic. But you'll see."

He did see. Sarah Lassiter had a better French accent than Chevalier, with none of the "zees" that lesser talents resorted to.

"There was nothing," she said, her lower lip showing a hint of a Gallic pout. "No warning. I was hit—*boom*—and never saw it coming."

Huston was fascinated. It took an effort to regain his focus. "Did you happen to notice Jill Baker? She's in

195

your class, isn't she?"

Sarah considered it. "She was there, yes, but not close-by."

"Did you see whether she was looking at your teacher?"

"*Oui.* They were looking at each other."

Huston felt a charge of excitement. "For how long?"

"I'm sorry?"

"Miss Appleton was walking toward the school. You and several other children, including Jill, were on the steps. When did they see each other, and for how long were they looking in each other's eyes?"

For the first time, the girl appeared troubled, a play of emotion on her face. "It wasn't long," she said, all trace of an accent vanished. "I counted to ten. That's about how long it takes her."

"Who?"

"Jill." She brushed her hair back from her face. "She's a witch, you know."

Thirty-Two

Since he'd missed his walk that morning, Mr. Rafferty decided to take one after dinner. His digestion wasn't what it used to be, and maybe a nice long stroll would settle his stomach.

Actually, he'd felt a mite sour all day, and it probably was unfair to blame it on the manicotti he'd had for supper, even though every time he put his fork to it, he imagined that beneath the tomato sauce he was cutting into short lengths of intestines which were filled with plump, wriggling maggots.

"An old fool," he said to himself as he maneuvered down the front porch steps. The path from his door to the sidewalk was strewn with the white rock from around the rose bushes, and he frowned. "Damn dogs."

He'd been joking the other night when he'd suggested to Georgia Baker that the dogs be shot—one of the privileges of age was being able to make outrageous statements without being challenged—but now he wasn't so sure.

They all might be better off if someone rounded up the beasts.

When the county Animal Control officers had come this afternoon to remove the dead dog's body, the spine had broken as they were lifting it up, and with a sound reminiscent of corn being husked, the carcass had broken in two.

Disgusting, he thought. It was enough to give anyone nightmares.

The night was still ahead, but coming closer. The sun was down and twilight was fading.

Rafferty turned left when he reached the sidewalk, and saw Jill Baker and another girl standing at the edge of the Baker lawn, looking at something Jill was holding in her hand.

It was unusual to see little Jill with a friend; the child was a loner. She didn't seem to mind it, either, or at least that was the impression he had.

"Mr. Rafferty," she said when she noticed he was coming in their direction. She closed her hand and held it behind her back.

"Evening," he said cordially. He peered at the other girl but didn't recognize her. "Hello?"

"This is my cousin Katy," Jill said.

Cousin Katy wasn't nearly as pretty as Jill, but her smile was infectious and he found himself grinning back. "Nice to meet you, Katy. Come for a visit?"

The girl nodded, her pony-tail bouncing. "I'm from LA. Hollywood, really."

"You're a long way from home," he said, making conversation. "How do you like our little town so far?"

"Okay, I guess."

"Well, it takes some getting used to, the quiet and all. But you can walk the streets at night and be as safe as if you were in your own bed and tucked in for the night."

"Why would you want to?" the girl asked.

"What?"

"Why would you want to walk the streets at night? What's there to see?"

Nonplussed, he shook his head. "Uh huh. I'd best be

on my way. Say hello to your mother for me."

When he was a few yards distant he heard them whispering and gave a look over his shoulder.

Their heads were together, and again they were looking at an object of some kind in Jill's outstretched hand. The light was too dim for him to be sure, but he thought it was nothing more than a lump of clay.

"Kids," he said. It didn't take much to amuse them.

The air was so invigorating that he walked far beyond his usual turning back place. It was a shame he hadn't had time to go over to the hospital and retrieve his cane, but he was doing fine without it.

Darkness had descended, and there was only a sliver of moon, but the road was lighted at intervals, and when walking through the shadows he could always look ahead to a pool of that light.

There were almost no cars out, perhaps one passing every ten minutes or so.

What with the dark and the silence, he could almost believe that he'd gone back in time, that he was twenty years old again, walking to town for a church social.

Of course, the roads hadn't been paved, just dirt that developed ruts in the spring when the snow thawed and created clouds of dust during the late summer when there's been no rain.

A car pass you by on a dirt road in August and you had something to show for it; he could still remember the smell of it in his nose, the taste and gritty feel of it in his mouth.

Hell, he used to beat himself silly trying to brush it from his clothes.

Those were the days.

Progress, they said, had made life better for all of them, but to his way of thinking, he'd rather inhale a little dirt from a road that was too pot-holed on which to drive more than fifteen miles an hour, than suck up a lung full of exhaust from hundreds of thousands of cars doing eighty on a twelve-lane freeway.

Well, never mind. It wasn't his problem.

A few more years and he'd be dust. And when the planet died and the earth was bare, it could be that a whirlwind would uncover his final resting place and lift *him* into the air.

He wouldn't mind that at all.

It had been a good while since he'd passed the last light and he hadn't yet come upon another, so he decided that it was time that he turn around and head back.

He was surprised when he turned. He couldn't see any light at all.

The sidewalk had long since stopped and he'd been walking along the paved shoulder of the road. He crossed the empty road to the other side so if a car approached he'd be facing it.

The only people who drove this far out were teen-age couples looking for a place to park, and heaven forbid the guy be copping a feel and thus distracted, weave out of the lane and into Rafferty.

He'd been willing to die in two World Wars, but he'd be damned if he'd sacrifice his life upon the altar of raging hormones.

He walked and walked on, getting tired now, his old stringy muscles threatening to put a hitch in his get-a-long. But at least he could see a light now, a dim glowing in the distance, maybe a half a mile away.

With something to fix on, he tried to pick up his pace, and his lungs labored from the effort, so that at first he didn't hear anything but his own breathing.

Until something moved across the road in front of him,

and disappeared into the blackness to his left.

Rafferty stopped to listen.

Rustling sounds, the kind an animal makes running through dry brush.

More than one animal, he thought.

The light beckoned him, and after a moment he resumed walking. Whatever animals were out here probably would be more frightened of him than he was of them. Could be a family of possum, except that the glimpse he'd gotten of them seemed bigger.

Like dogs. He stopped a second time.

Rafferty swallowed, his throat feeling ragged from his exertions. For the first time in a long time, he felt fear.

Don't let them know you're afraid. They can smell it on you.

He knew he couldn't continue to just stand there. His best bet was to reach the light; it wouldn't keep the dogs from attacking if they were going to, but at least he'd be able to see them.

He lowered his head slightly—some animals took eye contact as a direct challenge—and started off again, keeping a measured pace.

Behind him, he heard the telltale click of their claws on the pavement.

There was no hope of out-running them, and he refused to even try. Better to save his energy for fighting them off, if it came to that.

It went on that way, he walking steadily, they following behind. The light grew nearer, until at last he was in its circle.

Rafferty stumbled to the light-pole and wrapped one arm around it to hold himself up.

For a moment he closed his eyes, thankful to have made it, but when he opened them he saw that the animals—indeed dogs of a kind—had surrounded him.

"Get away," he said and made a shooing motion with

one hand. "Scat."

One of the creatures began to growl deep in its throat, and Rafferty braced himself for what he knew was to come.

The first to attack sunk yellowed teeth in the old man's upper leg, and Rafferty could only beat feebly at its head as warm blood poured out of the wound and down his thigh. The second caught his right wrist in its mouth and yanked.

He fell to the pavement and heard the crack of bone in his hip.

None of the wounds they'd inflicted yet were mortal, but Rafferty knew he would not survive this, even if the animals tired of the attack. Eighty-odd years of living had made him stubborn and he didn't want them to have the thrill of the kill, so he did the only thing he could.

He closed his eyes and died.

Thirty-Three

"God!" Cheryl Appleton cried, and sat straight up in bed. Her heart beat so hard she thought it might burst, and she placed one hand on her chest.

"What's wrong?" a voice asked.

She saw that a nurse was standing in the doorway, and for a moment she was confused—why was there a nurse in her bedroom?—until the dream cleared from her mind and she remembered that she was in the hospital.

The nurse was looking at her peculiarly.

"A dream," she said. "I had a bad dream."

"I don't wonder." The nurse came into the room, a small silver tray in her hand. Several tiny white paper cups were on the tray, and the nurse selected one which she handed to Cheryl. "Your pain medication."

Cheryl took it with a sip of warm water from the cup on her bedside table.

"What do you mean," she asked after swallowing, "you don't wonder?"

"It happens all the time." The nurse crumpled the paper cup and tossed it in the trash. "People injured in an accident often dream about the circumstances leading up to the moment they were hurt. And it usually results in a rude awakening."

"I wasn't dreaming about myself," Cheryl said.

"Oh? Then it has to be the moment you get the bill for all this, right?"

"No." She took another taste of water; the pill had left a bitter taste.

Or maybe it was the dream.

"No? Well, the day of reckoning will come," the nurse said cheerfully. "Is there anything else you need before I go?"

She shook her head and winced at the pain the movement had elicited in her neck. "Thank you."

The nurse left and Cheryl eased back down on the bed. Although the pain wasn't as bad as yesterday, she still hurt all over. As difficult as she found it simply to lie down, she wondered how had she sat up that abruptly without killing herself?

Fright, she supposed. The dream had scared her beyond her pain.

If dreams were based on subconscious thought, what had she been thinking to produce something as wrenching as an old man being savaged by wild dogs?

Maybe it was a side effect of the pain medication. If so, she was sorry she'd taken any.

Even though she'd slept all day, she was beginning to drift off again when someone tapped at the door.

"Miss Appleton? Are you awake?"

I am now, she thought, and opened her eyes.

The man at the door was attractive enough for her to suddenly be aware of the fact that she hadn't brushed her hair—or her teeth—since yesterday. A couple of inches shy of six feet, blond hair, brown eyes, and nicely dressed in dark slacks and a patterned ski sweater.

"Yes," she said. "I'm awake."

204

He came into the room and stood near the foot of her bed.

"I'm Doctor Huston—"

"Oh no," she said, "not another one."

"Another what?"

She pulled the covers up to her neck, feeling all at once exposed. Vulnerable. And mad. "I don't have to talk to you. I'm *not* crazy."

"I never—"

"Tell Mr. Barry 'nice try,' but I'm not talking to you or any other psychiatrist. I already told the jerk he sent by earlier to take a hike, and now I'm telling you. I know my rights, and I don't have to submit to a psychiatric evaluation for Barry or the school board."

"I'm not a psychiatrist," he said.

"Psychiatrist, psychologist, what's the difference? Oh, I know there is a difference—I don't mean to insult your profession—but I don't need my head examined. So get out before I call the nurse."

"Really, Miss Appleton, I'm not a psychologist either. I'm a medical doctor."

"I have a medical doctor."

He held up a hand to silence her. "I think you misunderstand. I'm not here to examine you, physically or emotionally. No one's sent me. I only want to talk to you about Jill Baker."

The name brought her up short and Cheryl narrowed her eyes. "What about her?"

"That's what I'm here to ask you. What about Jill Baker?"

She shook her head. "Why do you think I could tell you anything?"

"Because something happened yesterday between you and her . . ."

He'd paused, apparently to give her a chance to

complete his thought, but she said nothing. Experience had made her cautious; he would have to convince her that this was more than a plan by Mr. Barry to trick her into saying something for which she'd be sorry.

"I talked to Sarah Lassiter today."

"So?"

"She told me that you were looking at Jill Baker when you . . . when the accident happened."

"When I stepped in front of the bus, you mean."

"Did you, Miss Appleton? Did you knowingly step in front of that bus?"

There was an intensity in his eyes that she found disturbing, but she couldn't look away. He was asking essentially if she'd tried to kill herself, which he would do if Barry had sent him. On the other hand, if he'd spoken to Sarah about her and Jill, perhaps he knew something about what had happened beyond the mere details contained in the police report.

If that were the case, she wanted to know. Or rather, she *had* to know.

"I did not," she said finally.

"You were pushed?"

She wet her lips nervously, and glanced at the door which was standing open.

Without a word, he went to the door and closed it.

"I wouldn't say pushed," she said cautiously. "There was no sense of force."

Dr. Huston said nothing, but by his watchful silence she knew that he would not think her crazy for saying what she was going to say.

She took a deep breath. Once it was said, there was no turning back; she'd step into the *Twilight Zone*.

"It was more like being *drawn*."

All he did was nod.

"It was as if . . . as if she were a magnet, and I had a

metal core?"

"You couldn't resist?"

"I didn't want to."

"Even though—"

"Even though I saw the bus out of the corner of my eye and knew it was going to hit me."

"And all this time you were looking at each other?"

"Yes." She shivered, remembering the child's cool gaze. "Up to the moment of . . . impact."

"What happened then? Do you recall?"

"Not really. To be honest with you, I'm a coward. When I saw that the bus was going to . . . was not going to miss me, I blacked out."

"I see."

"I wish I did."

"Miss Appleton—"

"Call me Cheryl. If you're not the enemy, we might as well be friends."

"Cheryl," he said, and smiled. "I know this may sound odd to you, but I've been watching Jill for a long time, and one of the things I know about her is that she usually does these things to kids her own age. In fact, because you're an adult, I didn't originally consider you to be a victim. I thought either Sarah was the target and you were somehow swept in, or that it was a genuine accident."

"What made you change your mind?"

"A number of things. First, the fact that Jill herself fainted at the time of the incident—"

"So that's why she was here." At his questioning look, she added: "I saw her in the emergency room. I didn't know anything had happened to her. I don't mind telling you, it scared me half to death. I thought . . ."

"That she'd come to finish what she'd started?"

"Yes." The memory of her own helplessness was

still fresh in her mind. "But she didn't. I don't know why."

"I think I do. There's a limit to her abilities. Doing what she did to you took her to that limit, and she had to recharge."

Cheryl considered that. "So she knocked herself out for me. Should I be flattered?"

He smiled thinly. "No, frightened, because her attack on you is evidence that she's stretching."

"Getting stronger?"

"Absolutely. I'm not sure how she does what she does—what you describe could have been a form of mind control or simple kinetics—but the fact that all of a sudden she is trying her powers on adults indicates that she's no longer content with the status quo."

"Which is?"

"Terrorizing the kids in this town."

"Oh God." She thought of Kevin's arm and grimaced. "But why? Why would she do that?"

"I don't know. Practice, maybe. I'm not sure it matters at this point."

Cheryl felt sick to her stomach, imagining what kind of mind it would take to consider breaking bones and inflicting pain as "practice."

"What is she?" she whispered.

"I'll be damned if I know, and I've had seven years to find out."

"Seven *years?*"

"I'm responsible for all of this," he said, and Cheryl heard the anguish in his voice. "I let it go on too long because I didn't have the nerve to stop it."

She could think of nothing to say.

He began to talk, almost in a monotone, and she listened in stunned silence as he described delivering a baby girl on a stormy night. Beads of sweat appeared on his brow as he talked.

"I brought her into this world," he concluded, "and set her loose."

"But you didn't know, you *couldn't*. Not a newborn baby."

"I should have. The first couple who adopted her refused to keep her. They wouldn't talk to me at first, but when I kept showing up on their doorstep, year after year, they finally gave in."

"What did they say?"

"The woman was alone at home with the baby for the first time, and she was trying to change a diaper when she accidentally stuck Jill. A pinprick, but . . . this black stuff, the same thing I'd seen, came out of Jill's mouth and nearly suffocated the mother. She was unconscious on the floor when her husband came home."

"They didn't tell anyone?"

"They thought no one would believe them. The woman had a history of epilepsy, and they were afraid that if they told the truth the adoption agency would either think she was crazy, or think that she'd fudged on her medication and wasn't fit to care for a child. They still wanted a baby, but not Jill."

"You said first couples. Were there others?"

"One other before the Bakers adopted her. Those folks barely kept her a full day. They were on the doorstep waiting for the agency to open to give her back."

"Did they explain why?"

"The official version is they decided they really wanted to hold out for a little boy."

"What about unofficially?"

"They were divorced by the time I found them. He told me he had nothing to say, but she was a little more forthcoming. Apparently they had a couple of exotic birds, which had free run of the house. I guess the birds must have startled the baby."

"She killed them?"

He nodded. "I think the woman witnessed it, but she refused to admit to that. She's still scared. And childless."

"I don't blame her. But how did the Bakers manage all these years?"

"I'm not sure, except that Georgia is a good mother. Maybe she never felt threatened once she was in their home. She needed someone to take care of her needs."

"It's so awful," Cheryl said. "Talking about her as if she's some kind of monster—"

"She is. Make no mistake about that. She may look like a pretty little girl, but she would have killed you yesterday if she could."

"So, what do we do?"

"We have to stop her before she gets any stronger. She hasn't killed yet, but it's only a matter of time before she does."

"Do you realize what you're saying?"

He shook his head. "The question is, do *you* realize what I'm saying?"

"I . . . you . . ." The words refused to come.

"We have to destroy her, and soon. If I'm not mistaken, something is *building*. She's doing things in front of witnesses, which she hasn't before. The night fogs we've been having . . . I checked with the meteorology service and not only are there no reasons for them, they don't show up on the satellite map."

"How is that possible?"

"I have no idea. Then there are the dogs. It could be they've been attracted by what she's doing. It's possible they're here as scavengers, and they're waiting for her to play out her hand."

Cheryl nodded mutely and wrapped her arms around herself, all at once chilled to the bone.

"What I'm getting to is, I can't do this alone. Will you help me?"

"How can I? I can't get out of this bed."

"You can act as bait," he said quietly.

Thirty-Four

"What's all the laughing about?" Georgia asked with a smile when Katy came into the kitchen. "What are you two doing back there?"

"Nothing."

Bev shook a finger at her daughter. "Katy, you know better. That's not an answer."

"Jill is showing me some tricks," Katy said, and curtsied.

"Tricks?" Georgia raised her eyebrows at Bev. "Jill doesn't know any tricks."

"Yes she does. Can we have a can of soda, Aunt Georgia?"

"Help yourself."

"Thanks."

Georgia waited until Katy left and then sighed. "Were we ever that age?"

"Must have been." Bev took a pretzel from the bowl and broke off one of the twists. "Although you were eight when I was born, so we weren't that age together."

"They sure seem to be having fun. I'm glad they're getting along so well."

"So am I, but if they could get along a little quieter it would suit me fine. They must be measuring 5.8 on the

213

Richter scale."

Georgia tried to remember when she'd last heard so much laughter coming from her daughter's room, and then realized she never had.

Jill wasn't one to invite her school friends to the house.

"Anyway," Bev said, "I hope they run down pretty soon, or we're not going to get any sleep tonight."

"You know, I wouldn't mind."

"You're crazy." Bev grabbed Georgia's glass and sniffed at it. "What're you drinking, to make you say crazy things like that?"

"Ice tea, same as you." She put her elbow on the table and cupped her face in her hands. "I love to listen to them laugh."

"You've got to get out more. I think living in the sticks has affected your brain."

"Well, maybe that'll change."

"What are you talking about?"

Georgia hesitated. "I may not be living in Winslow much longer."

"Ah, now we're getting to it." Bev sat back in her chair and drummed her fingers on the table. "Okay, spill it."

"I'm thinking of taking Jill and leaving. I know I can get a job in another town. I'm only short six units on my degree, and if I could finish the requirements, I could even get a better job."

"Sounds great." She hesitated and took another pretzel, frowning as she removed the salt crystals from it. "Does Dave know you're planning on leaving him?"

"No."

"How do you think he'll take it?"

"Well I guess that depends."

"On what?"

"On how soon he notices I'm gone," she said, and knew her smile was bitter.

"That bad, huh?"

She nodded, then reached up to massage her neck. The tension had knotted the muscles to the point that it hurt to rub them.

"At work today I was trying to figure you how much time we've spent together in the last few months. It works out to be about ten minutes a day, not counting sleeping in the same bed—"

"Which is all you do in bed, right?"

"Right."

"It figures." Bev popped the pretzel in her mouth.

"Anyway, I've thought it out from every angle, and I'm not getting anything out of this marriage. So maybe *I* should be getting out of this marriage."

"You know, I'll be honest. I've wondered lots of times why you were still with him."

Georgia looked at her sister curiously. "You never did like him, did you?"

"No, I surely didn't."

"Would you mind telling me why?"

"Oh no! I'm not *that* honest. You might change your mind, kiss and make up, and then where'd I be?"

"I'm not going to change my mind," Georgia said.

"We'll see. But you say you've figured every angle, I assume that includes—"

Georgia held up a hand to stop her. "I've already had the money lecture today."

"I'm not thinking of the money. If I can get by on what I make working temp jobs, you'll be fine. It's the security thing I'm wondering about."

"Security?"

"Having him around. Maybe he's not everything you ever wanted in a husband, but he's here—"

"Sort of," Georgia corrected.

"Okay, maybe he's not *physically* here a lot of the time, but his clothes are in the closet, his razor's in the

215

bathroom, the toilet seat is up when you go to use it in the middle of the night. He's here in the sense that you're not living alone."

"Ten minutes a day, Bev. If I can find something else to do for those ten minutes when I'd be with Dave, I don't think I'll even miss him."

Bev shook her head. "You always miss them, no matter what kind of bastards they were. Sort of the way you miss a tooth that's been pulled. It might have been hurting you so bad you couldn't stand it, but when it's gone, you tongue keeps probing that hole."

"Are you trying to talk me out of it?"

"Hell no. If you really want to go, say the word. I'll help you pack up your and Jill's stuff, we can load the cars, and be out of here before morning. All I'm saying is, be sure."

"I *am* sure."

"I hope so. I'm not going to pretend to be an authority on marriage, because I've never been married, obviously, but I know in any relationship there is a point of no return, and you cross it at your own risk. And I mean to tell you, it can be scary as hell—"

"I know."

Bev looked doubtful. "I'm not sure you do. No matter what's going on between two people, when it's over, there will come a moment when it hits you that you're alone. It's an empty feeling."

Georgia said nothing, but that feeling had already come. She'd spent her lunch hour in the employee restroom literally shaking from the shock of having to come to the only decision she felt she could make.

"If you're ready, though, I'm here for you. If you want to come down to LA, you can stay with Katy and me until you get settled. We'd be living in close quarters, but what the hell. We're family."

The thought of driving away on impulse was both

216

heady and sobering. Georgia reached across the table and took her sister's hand.

"I wish we could go tonight, but there are some things I have to take care of first. And I've got to do this in a way that's the least painful for Jill—"

"And for you," Bev interrupted. "You have to think of yourself here, too. Now isn't the time to be selfless."

"Don't worry about me." Georgia squeezed her hand. "Remember, I'm the big sister."

"Not so big that you can't cry. No one's ever so big that they can't cry."

Thirty-Five

Katy was wide awake.

The house had been quiet for at least an hour, and Jill was sleeping soundly, but whether it was being in a strange bed or the things that she'd seen today, Katy wasn't able to get to sleep.

She'd tried lying on her stomach, her back, on her right side with her legs curled tight, on her left side with her legs straight out.

She'd tried thinking the same word over and over, trying to induce a kind of trance. She counted backwards from one hundred. She'd tried closing her eyes and crossing them, which sometimes made her dizzy but often had the effect of making her drowsy as well.

Even though she didn't quite get what doing one had to do with attaining the other, she counted sheep.

Nothing worked.

She stared at the ceiling, hands behind her head, and wondered how Jill did the things she did.

Sleight of hand, she supposed. Once when her mother had worked a full week as a movie extra and they were flush, they'd gone with a bunch of her mom's friends to celebrate their good fortune at the Magic Castle.

They'd been ensconced in a small private dining room

219

with their own waiter and a chef who'd prepared several flamed dishes, including Cherries Jubilee and the best cooked carrots she'd ever tasted.

Before, during and after dinner, they were entertained by magicians.

A lot of the tricks they performed, she'd seen before on television, but she'd been intrigued at seeing them done up close.

Try as she might, though, she hadn't been able to catch the magicians at their wiles. As carefully as she watched their hands, she couldn't see past the carefully crafted illusion.

She understood magicians were masters at misdirection, but she'd always considered herself, a child of Hollywood, the world capital of make-believe, as being wise to their guise.

But if those guys were good, her cousin was great.

So great that if *she* were David Copperfield, she'd start looking for another line of work.

Copperfield performed with a lot of flash and dazzle, but she'd never seen him turn a solid to liquid and then back again.

Katy sat up in bed and looked toward her sleeping cousin.

"Jill," she whispered. "Jill?"

Her cousin didn't stir.

Katy turned the covers aside and slipped out of bed. She walked on tiptoe to the small bedside table where Jill kept the wooden box of buttons.

The table drawer stuck a bit—she'd pulled it out crookedly—and squeaked.

She held her breath, waiting to see if Jill would awaken. When she didn't, Katy eased the drawer further open and reached in for the box.

It felt surprisingly heavy in her hands, most likely from the weight of its secret compartment, she supposed, and the weight of the liquid, of course.

She left the drawer standing open so that it would be easier to return the box, started toward her bed, but then hesitated.

The thing was, she needed light to examine the box. Even if she raised the window shade by the bed, there was almost no moon out tonight, and she wouldn't be able to see clearly enough to check for hidden panels or levers or whatever the mechanism was that controlled the box.

Standing on the bare floor was making her feet cold, and she lifted one foot to rub it against the warm material of her pajama leg.

Jill sighed in her sleep and turned over.

That was enough impetus.

As her mother always said, "He who hesitates, sits through the red light twice."

Katy reached the door without making any noise, and was relieved to find that it hadn't been fully closed. She put a finger on the latch bolt to keep it from clicking when it came free of the striker plate, and after that she was home free.

She turned on the bathroom light and the fan, then turned on the faucet to help cover the sounds of her quest. She took a face towel and spread it on the counter, in case the liquid inside spilled as she was trying to open it, and put the box down.

She thought it odd that the box wasn't painted or carved the way most magic devices were. If it belonged to her, she'd paint it black and gold, and have a sprinkling of stars across the lid.

At the very least she'd want it lined in velvet, the better to show off the first stage of the trick.

Katy leaned over so the box was on eye level, and studied the front panel. There was a simple metal clasp that held the box shut, and she used her thumbnail to undo it.

With the lid still closed, she ran her fingers over the exterior of the box, thinking that she might feel what she couldn't see.

No such luck; the wood had been sanded completely smooth and hadn't even the tiniest indentation.

Katy lifted her eyebrows at her reflection in the mirror which looked as baffled as she did.

Maybe, she thought, the trick was on the inside.

She opened the lid and after a moment, frowned. Even though it was filled with buttons, she could see that there wasn't enough thickness to the box to contain an inner panel of some kind.

Katy dipped her fingers into the buttons, feeling beneath them for a scored area on the bottom. The wood on the inside felt slippery but unyielding.

"How did she do that?" Katy whispered.

An optical illusion, obviously, but Katy had been standing close by Jill's side when her cousin had passed her right hand through the buttons, filtering them through her fingers, until somehow, they'd turned to a silvery-black liquid before her eyes.

A drop of the liquid had fallen to the floor, and when she'd glanced down, it had transformed into an ordinary gray button. Four holes, flat on one side, indented on the other. She'd picked it up, and it was solid, if slightly warm to the touch.

When she'd looked at Jill in amazement, the younger girl had smiled, holding out the box so she could see.

All of the buttons had returned to their original form.

Katy had cupped her hands so that Jill could fill them with buttons. They, too, were warm.

Then Jill had selected one, held it between her thumb and forefinger so that Katy could see it—it was a red one—and in an instant it had vanished.

There was no doubt about it, Katy thought; her cousin was uniquely talented.

Magical, in a word.

She only wished she could figure out how the kid had gotten to be that way.

Jill had burrowed completely under the covers when Katy returned to the room.

She gently eased the box into the drawer and slowly, slowly pushed the drawer closed. Not even a squeak this time, thank goodness.

Back in bed, Katy yawned and hugged the pillow to her. The sheets had cooled and she felt pleasantly shivery and tired.

As she was about to close her eyes, a car drove by and the reflected headlights brightened the room, and she thought she saw a dark mass of some kind hovering above her cousin's bed.

She blinked several times, and it faded.

Or maybe it hadn't been there at all.

Her imagination was starting to get the best of her, Katy thought, and fell asleep.

Sunday

Thirty-Six

Noah Huston arrived back in Winslow shortly before daybreak after having driven to Los Angeles for supplies he knew he couldn't get at the small hospital. Or rather, couldn't ask for.

Why, they would wonder, did he need curare?

The drug, used in anesthesia, facilitated skeletal muscular relaxation, inducing paralysis within minutes by blocking nerve impulses to the muscles at the myoneural junction.

It did not render the patient unconscious, nor did it have any effect on pain.

The preferred method of administration was intravenously, since intramuscular injection produced unpredictable results. Rapid infusion of the drug into the system was dangerous but a small dose given fast could paralyze the patient in seconds.

Respiratory depression secondary to increased levels of histamine was a potential complication, with bronchospasm and paralysis of the muscles necessary to breathe. Hypotension was also a possibility.

Finally, the drug could be lethal; it an overdose was given, there was no antidote, no antagonist to reverse its effects.

Used correctly, curare, or more accurately turbo-curarine chloride, was a powerful medical tool.

And the way he intended to use it?

He couldn't bring himself to say the word, but he knew what most people would call it.

Huston pulled into the driveway and shut the engine off. There was a humming in his ears—too many hours spent on the road—and he had a dull ache in the small of his back.

As he got out of the car, he glanced across the street at the Baker house, but all was still. That wasn't unusual for a Sunday morning.

The entire neighborhood tended to sleep on Sundays, with the exception of Mr. Rafferty. Case in point, the only sign of anyone being up yet was the light he could see at the back of the old man's house.

A couple of times over the years he'd accepted Rafferty's invitations for morning coffee, and he remembered quite well the sunny kitchen, fragrant with the scent of fresh-ground coffee and cinnamon rolls.

The old guy was lonely, although he'd never admit it, Huston thought.

There were too many hours in a day to fill, Rafferty had told him once, even in a town full of retired folks like himself.

"I don't care for lawn games," the old man had said. "Never understood bridge. Chess is too highfalutin' by half. And if I never hear another joker call a square dance I will die a happy man."

Instead of participating in the social activities for the older set, Rafferty had kept himself busy volunteering at the hospital, tending his yard, and keeping a watchful eye on his neighborhood.

A nice old guy, to be sure.

Huston glanced at his watch, wondering if it was too early to be knocking on a neighbor's door. Six a.m.? He'd probably be welcomed.

But no, he thought, I wouldn't be fit company.

In truth, he was so exhausted that he wanted nothing more than a hot shower and eight hours of uninterrupted sleep.

And he couldn't fool himself; the only reason he was even considering paying a call on the old gent was to put a buffer of sorts between himself and his conscience. He'd been alone with his thoughts for too many hours.

Another time, he thought, when all of this is over.

Thirty-Seven

After a few missed guesses, Beverly located the coffee in her sister's kitchen cupboard and set about making a pot. As luck would have it, Georgia's coffeemaker was the same model as the one she had at home.

Great minds, she thought.

More likely Georgia had shopped carefully for the perfect machine to meet her family's needs, while personally, she'd bought the first one she found on sale.

Actually, that pretty much summed up their lives.

Georgia was deliberate and thorough; she was impulsive and scattered.

Georgia had married and set out to have a family; she'd gotten pregnant and had fought tooth and nail to keep from being pushed into marriage.

Georgia, the librarian, lived a quiet life in the little town of Winslow. Beverly, the actress, with her blinkers on, tried to merge into the fast lane in big bad Los Angeles.

Despite their differences in age and style, they'd always been friends. Although for a while there, back when she was so easily, accidentally pregnant and Georgia had been told by the specialists that she'd never have a child, things had gotten tense.

231

Georgia had never said anything, but sometimes Beverly could see it in her eyes:

Here I am, desperate to have a baby, and there you are, eighteen, unmarried, and pregnant.

There'd been a little jealousy, and even anger, between them, but the most beautiful baby gift she'd received was a hand-crocheted blanket from her sister.

Katy still had the blanket. All on her own, she'd folded it in half, sewn the sides together, stuffed it with foam she'd bought from a notions store, and made it into a pillow for her bed.

It was odd that Katy hadn't brought it with her. Of course, they'd been in a hurry to leave.

Since Katy had decided to stay on here for the week, Beverly thought she'd need the pillow to keep her company. Unless she got a better offer?

There was always Roger . . .

"Good morning."

She turned from the counter. Dave stood in the doorway, running a hand through sleep-tousled hair.

"You're up early," he said. "Are you having coffee or just warming yourself on the pot?"

"Oh, is it finished?" She looked at the pot which was indeed full.

Dave laughed. He got two mugs from a shelf and handed her one. "Woolgathering?"

She didn't answer, but moved to one side as he poured his coffee. His nearness disturbed her, and not in a pleasant way.

"A little touchy, aren't we?" he asked.

"What?"

"I don't bite."

Beverly shook her head, as though she missed his meaning, and filled her mug. "Is Georgia awake?"

"Sunday's the only day of the week she can sleep late. She usually takes full advantage of it." He went to sit at

232

the table.

Beverly could feel him watching her as she crossed the room and took a carton of milk from the refrigerator. She spilled a little adding it to her coffee and cursed under her breath.

"So," she said, wiping the milk up with a paper towel, "Georgia tells me you're working long hours at the restaurant."

"That's an understatement."

"But it's going well?"

"You might say that." He stretched his legs out in front of him. "Why don't you sit down, Beverly?"

She would have to walk around him if she wanted to sit at the table. "This is fine," she said, and leaned against the counter.

"Something bothering you?"

"No. Why do you ask?"

The smile was back, cool and insinuating. "I don't know. You're acting funny, like you're nervous about being alone with me."

"Don't flatter yourself." She took a sip of coffee, aware that she was doing it for the sole purpose of hiding her expression from him.

"Then what's the problem? Ever since I came in, you've been skittish—"

"Why are we having this conversation?" She frowned into her coffee which was still too hot to really drink. "I thought we were talking about the restaurant."

He arched an eyebrow. "All right. If you insist. What about the restaurant? You want to know about the most recent quarterly report? Maybe what the estimated payroll is for this year? Or would you like to discuss the specifications of the new computerized cash register I'm thinking of buying."

"Don't be sarcastic."

He held out his hands, palms up. "You want to talk

233

business, I'll talk business."

"What I *don't* want to talk about, Dave, is anything personal."

"Why not? You're my sister-in-law. We're related. Why shouldn't we talk about our personal lives?"

"Because I'm not going to."

Dave moved his legs, as though getting ready to stand, and she shied toward the door.

"Don't run," he said, and laughed. "Why are you always running?"

His laughter infuriated her and that stopped her cold. "You're a real bastard, aren't you?"

"I don't know, Beverly. It seems to me that you have more experience with bastards than I do."

"You son of a—" She closed her eyes, fighting the urge to throw hot coffee in his face. She couldn't do it, no matter how good it might make her feel, because then she'd have to explain to Georgia, and that was something she could never do.

"Why don't you leave me alone?" she asked, her throat tightening with frustration.

"You don't want me to."

His voice came from nearby and she opened her eyes. He was at arm's length, but he'd positioned himself between her and the door.

"Oh boy, you're wrong. I've never wanted anything to do with you."

"Never? Don't tell me you've forgotten?"

She felt the beginnings of a blush.

"No, I didn't think you had."

"I'm sorry Georgia ever married you."

"I'm sure you are."

Beverly wanted very much to say something that would take that smug expression off his face, but she had to respect her sister's confidences. "What the hell do you want?"

234

"For you to admit it," he said. "That's all I want. You admit that you were as much to blame for what happened as I was, and I'll never mention it again."

Beverly stared at him, trying to see past the cocky grin. Was this some kind of ruse? A little game he was playing?

"Come on, Bev," he said, his tone low and intimate. "There's no one here but us . . . and both of us know what really happened."

"Nothing goddamn happened!"

"But you wanted it to—"

Beverly slammed the coffee mug on the counter, and heard it break, but was out of the room before Dave could react.

She locked herself in the guest room, then stood there, uncertain what to do. After a moment, she crawled back into bed, clothes and all.

"Damn his eyes," she said.

She'd been fourteen when Georgia got married, but everyone said she looked older. Dressed in the pale blue satin bridesmaid's dress, she felt older.

The dress had been specially made for her, and it hugged her slender body like no other dress she'd ever worn. The neckline was daring, and showed the rise of her breasts along with a hint of white lace.

"You look beautiful," Georgia had said.

"Wow, so do you." She'd never seen her sister look so pretty and special as in her wedding gown. It was true what they said about brides, she thought, because Georgia's face did seem to glow.

"Would you do me a favor, honey?"

"Sure."

"Would you go downstairs and sneak me a glass of wine? I'm so damned nervous I can hardly stand it."

Beverly smiled at her sister's reflection in the mirror,

watching as she fussed with her veil. "If that's what you want . . . can I have a glass too?"

"I guess it wouldn't do any harm," Georgia said. "Just hurry."

Downstairs, she'd gone into the kitchen and found one of their mother's bottles—she and Georgia knew all of the hiding places—and poured each of them a glass. Because she was thirsty, she'd downed half of her glass and then refilled it before taking both up to Georgia's room.

On the way up, she'd had to sip a taste out of each glass to keep the wine from spilling. And when Georgia left to go down to the parlor to await the music, she finished what remained in her sister's glass.

By the time she preceeded her sister down the aisle, Beverly was more than a little intoxicated.

The party, held there at the house, went on and on. There was no end to the opportunities to drink. She toasted the bride and groom, sipped from unattended glasses, and by eight that night, she found she could barely stand.

Somehow, she found herself in the family room. The lights were off and she didn't bother to turn them on before crossing to the divan and sitting down.

"You too?" a voice said.

"Who is it?"

"Only the groom." He was sitting in her father's chair a few feet away from her, and he switched on one of the reading lamps. "Hi."

"God," she said, and giggled. "Weren't you on a wedding cake the last time I saw you?"

"No, that was a shorter guy."

"That's right. Much shorter. Much, much, much shorter."

"Are you okay, Beverly? You sound a little drunk."

"Not me. We don't get drunk in this family, don't you know that?"

Dave shook his head. "I guess I'll learn."

"Boy, will you." She leaned her head back against the cushion but it made her head spin. "Oh oh."

"What's wrong?"

"Shouldn't have done that." She got unsteadily to her feet. "I think the trick is to keep moving. 'Cause if you don't, the room will."

"Wait a minute—"

Dave got to her at about the time she fell off her high heels.

"Damn," she swore. His arms were around her, holding her. "You'd think I'd never worn heels before."

"Have you?"

"Ha! No. Maybe I'd better take them off. Hold onto me, so I don't fall."

"I've got you." His arms tightened around her.

She leaned to one side, and lifted one foot while reaching down with her hand. The shoe dropped to the floor. She repeated the process on the other side.

"There."

"There," he repeated.

Beverly leaned against him, her head on his chest. She could hear his heartbeat and feel the warmth of him. It was an incredibly comforting feeling, and she didn't want it to stop.

He seemed content to stand there holding her.

Gradually she became aware of other nice feelings; the pressure of his hands on her lower back, his breath against her hair, the very sturdiness of him.

"Beverly," he said.

"Hmm?"

"I'd better go. They'll be looking for me."

"No," she protested and tightened her arms around

237

his waist. How had her arms gotten to be around his waist?

"Come on."

"But . . . I haven't even got to kiss the groom yet. You can't go without a kiss."

His hands flexed against her back. "A kiss."

"Everyone gets to kiss the bride." She lifted her head from his chest and looked up at him. "I think it's only fair that somebody gets to kiss the groom."

"Do you now?"

She'd never realized before how gray his eyes were. Or how attractive he looked from this close. "I think it should be me," she said.

"Well," he said.

Before he could say no, she took her arms from around his waist, wrapped them around his neck, and raised up on her toes until their faces were even closer.

"I think you should—"

Beverly didn't let him finish what he was saying. She eliminated the distance between them, her mouth hungrily searching his.

Nothing else existed.

Now, remembering, all these years later, she could still feel the heat of him, imagine his arms around her, smell his aftershave, taste his mouth.

Beverly didn't really know who had stopped—she hoped it had been her—but later on, when she'd realized what they'd done and what they might have done, she'd started to hate David Baker.

The guilt she felt for her part in their embrace was alleviated somewhat by that hatred.

She wasn't blameless, by any means, but he had been the adult, and she, hardly more than a child. An intoxicated fourteen-year-old child, not even fully aware of what her body was able to feel.

It was easy to blame the wine, easy to blame him. Not so easy to deny those feelings. Or to forget who'd awakened them in her.

Beverly loved her sister, and she was going to miss having Katy with her, but she was very much looking forward to getting out of this town.

Thirty-Eight

"All the great weather we've been having and wouldn't you know it, today of all days, it's going to rain." Georgia turned from the window to look at Bev. "So much for our picnic."

"There'll be other days," her sister said.

"I know."

"If you come to LA, we can have a picnic in Griffith Park, or maybe on the beach."

"The beach?" Her eyes were drawn again to the dark clouds which seemed to almost boil in the sky. "That sounds like fun."

"Has Jill ever been to see the ocean?"

Georgia shook her head. "I wanted to take her, but something always came up."

"Then it's something to look forward to," Bev said. "I remember taking Katy for the first time. She'd only just started to walk, but when I took her shoes off, I guess she didn't like the feel of the sand. She absolutely refused to take a step. She stayed on the blanket all afternoon, with this huge frown on her face. Poor baby."

"Katy's a great kid." She was feeling a little melancholy—cloudy days did that to her sometimes—and she had to force a smile. "I'm glad she's staying."

241

"Georgia, I know that you have some kind of plan; you usually do. But don't you think you should reconsider, and all of us leave today?"

It struck Georgia that Beverly appeared tense this morning, in marked contrast to the ease of last night. "Is anything wrong?"

Bev sighed. "I wish you'd come with me, now."

"I can't. I have things I need to do."

"Such as?"

"Well, for starters I need to get some money from the bank."

"What? They've never heard of automated tellers up here?"

"And I wanted to talk to Mr. Cosgrove about Dad's will."

"Oh that."

"Yes that." She regarded her sister curiously. "I don't understand why you aren't more concerned."

"Because I'm not. It isn't that much money—"

"I think it comes to almost fifty thousand dollars," Georgia said.

"So what? It's here today and gone tomorrow. Look, I never cared about the money, and as far as I'm concerned it doesn't exist. Dad did what he did to get to me; if I don't give a damn, he lost."

"But I think he may have had a change of heart when he was in the hospital that last time. I think he may have revised his will—"

"Again," Bev inserted.

"Yes, again. I've held off letting Mr. Cosgrove settle the estate because I was sure we'd find a new codicil if we kept on looking."

Bev frowned. "I don't want his money, do you understand?"

"But why not? You could put it in a trust for Katy, for when she starts college."

242

"Don't be *logical*, for crying out loud."

That startled her, and she laughed. And laughed. And couldn't stop.

Bev looked annoyed. "Georgia . . ."

"I'm sorry," she said, gasping for air between fits of laughter. "It's just so absurd."

"What is?"

She held up a hand while she regained her composure. "There's no logic to it and it isn't at all like I'd planned. Or *any*one planned."

"No?"

"Dave wants the money and can't get it; you don't want anything to do with it and I'm trying to force it on you; and Dad probably thought leaving it all to me would drive a wedge between us, but instead I'm going to use the damn money to buy us a house."

"It won't buy much of a house in LA," Bev said, but Georgia noticed a hint of a smile.

"Who cares? We'll all live together, happily ever after."

While Bev was packing her things for the trip back to LA, Georgia took the phone into her bedroom and closed the door.

Everything was clear, now. She knew what she had to do.

She dug around in a drawer until she located her address book, then found Mr. Cosgrove's home phone number, which he'd given her all those months back when her father died.

She punched out the number quickly, before she had a chance to change her mind. There was a possibility he hadn't returned yet from his business trip—the office girl had told her he'd be back tomorrow—but she crossed her fingers for luck.

And was rewarded.

"Hello?" The attorney's voice was distinctly querulous.

"Mr. Cosgrove, this is Georgia Baker—"

"Don't tell me," he interrupted, "you've remembered an old steamer trunk your father left in storage in some out-of-the-way place like Montana?"

"No, it's—"

"You think he wrote a new will out on the back of an envelope on his way to Gettysburg?"

The lawyer seemed to delight in needling his clients. If he weren't the only lawyer in town, Georgia thought, he wouldn't have any.

"Mr. Cosgrove, I need to see you as soon as possible."

"Well, call my office."

"Wait! Don't hang up." Her hand tightened on the receiver. "Would it be all right if I came by this afternoon to talk to you?"

"This afternoon? At my home?"

"I know it's an unusual request, but it really is urgent."

"Urgent, that's what everyone says."

Georgia sensed that he was wavering; he hadn't slammed the phone down yet. "I won't take much of your time."

"I suppose, if you must. But I warn you, I'm not in the mood for another wild goose chase."

"Thank you, Mr. Cosgrove."

"Huh!" he said, and hung up the phone.

Outside, the rain started coming down.

Thirty-Nine

Murphy's law was in effect, the deputy figured; it started to rain at the precise moment he had to get out of the cruiser.

Fat drops splattered on his windshield, only a few at first but within a few seconds, the rain was pouring down. They beat out a rhythm on the roof of the car and if he didn't have to check out a foul odor report, the sound would have put him to sleep.

He needed a little sleep after last night.

God, that Tanya could kill a man with that finely-tooled body of hers.

Not that he was complaining; in a town where the average female resident was sixty years or older, young blood was a rarity, and he knew he was lucky to have been the first to catch the girl's eye. There were plenty of other guys who were more than willing, and in fact, were waiting in the wings.

But Tanya, bless her kinky little heart, liked men in uniform.

Better still, she liked to take the uniform off him. She liked his baton, the cuffs, and especially his gun. She practically begged to be frisked.

"Arrest me, officer," she'd said that first night. "I'll

go quietly."

She hadn't, though. He'd had to cover her mouth, and then things had *really* heated up.

What that girl could do . . .

"Whoa!" he said. Even thinking about her was enough to steam the windows of the patrol car. Time to get this show on the road.

"Patrol sixteen," he said into the microphone.

"Go ahead, sixteen," the dispatcher replied through static.

"I'm ten ninety-eight at Black Mountain."

"Ten-four, Sixteen, you're ten ninety-eight Black Mountain."

He stepped out of the car and into the storm. It wouldn't have surprised him any if the rain that landed on his skin had hissed and evaporated like drops of water in a hot iron skillet.

He went around to the trunk, got out his rain gear, and shrugged his way into the slicker. There were pants, similar to what the firemen wore, but they were more nuisance than help—they weighed a ton—and he left them folded in the trunk next to the first-aid kit and flares.

The deputy grabbed the portable Motorola, slipped his baton in the ring of his Sam Browne belt, glanced in either direction, then set off along the road.

There weren't any real landmarks out this way, and the person who'd called in had only said that he'd smelled something bad on Black Mountain Road between Lake Avenue and the old Sorghum place.

Not pinpoint accuracy; he had a good two mile stretch of road to cover.

When he'd caught the call, he'd asked the dispatcher why the guy who'd reported it hadn't been able to narrow down the site a bit more, and why the hell *he* hadn't investigated if it smelled so awful.

She reminded him that as an officer of the law, part of his job was to find the dead bodies, which was what most foul odor calls resulted from.

Probably somebody's pet got clipped by a car and crawled off in the bushes to die. No doubt this very minute, there was a little old blue-haired lady walking around, calling "Here kitty, kitty."

And, he thought, somewhere there was a bowl of Kitty's favorite food, waiting in a dish on the back porch of Kitty's house, an enticement to come home.

Oh well. If the county wanted to pay him to walk along a deserted road and sniff for road-kill, who was he to complain.

If something was dead and stinking, he'd find it sooner or later.

Oddly enough, he saw it before he smelled it.

Something red way back in the bushes, a good two hundred yards away from the road. It was bright red, too bright to be natural. A man-made color, like a piece of cloth or something.

He hoped very much that it wasn't what he thought it was.

He began to trudge through the tall grass and weeds toward the spot. The grass blades shimmered with beads of rainwater, and before he'd gone ten feet, the legs of his uniform pants were soaked through to the skin all the way up to his knees.

And he'd only gotten this uniform back from the dry cleaners two days ago.

"Shit."

He should have worn the damn pants to his rain gear.

"'Should-haves' don't fucking count," he said, disgusted. It was one of the Sergeant's favorite sayings, minus the expletive.

Here he was, out in the rain, messing up his uniform risking pneumonia, and missing a nap.

If one more bad thing happened, he'd have to reconsider his good mood, adjust his attitude accordingly, and kiss this one off as a rotten day.

It was a rotten day.

He didn't detect the odor until he was practically on top of the thing—maybe the rain had dampened that, too—but once he caught a whiff, he knew.

This was a human body.

He'd been a cop long enough to have learned that there was a subtle but distinct difference between the smell of human and animal remains during decomposition. Animals had more of a gamey odor; human, almost sickly sweet.

Size also was a factor, with the larger body mass exuding the more powerful . . . fragrance? He started breathing through his mouth to save his nose.

Automatically, he brought the radio up and checked in with dispatch, giving his approximate location, and requesting a second unit be sent. "And notify the county coroner, would you?"

"Ten-four," the dispatcher said. "Be advised, ETA is five to ten for back-up."

He acknowledged and signed off.

Rain pelted down on him, harder all of a sudden, icy drops finding their way beneath the collar of his rain slicker and down his back.

He took a few careful steps forward, until he could see part of what lay in the grass.

The red that had attracted his attention from the road proved to be a sweater. A man's cardigan, he thought, but he couldn't tell for sure.

The body could have been of either sex; it had been

savaged until it didn't much resemble a human. However it had died, the animals had been at it, and there were huge chunks of flesh ripped out of the torso. The right arm had been torn clean away. The left hand was missing. Loops of intestine had been pulled from the abdominal cavity and spilled into the dirt.

The face was pretty much gone, except for the lower jaw which incongruously sported a set of dentures.

They smiled at him amid the carnage, a rather grisly happy face. A pair of eyeglasses clung to the left ear, the lenses shattered.

Someone or something had done a number on this poor soul.

His own stomach twisted, but he wasn't a rookie and no one was going to find him puking his guts up.

There were guts-a-plenty as it was.

Since he had no way of knowing what the means of death had been, his duty was to preserve what might be a crime scene. To that end, he decided to go no closer, but to walk a circle around the body after first visually inspecting the area to see if he could determine whether there were tracks leading to or away from where it lay.

The only tracks he saw were his own.

He moved carefully, slowly, inspecting the ground before each step. It took him several minutes to complete his sweep and the only thing he found was a small patch of bloodied ground.

He hunkered down for a closer look. Bone fragments and shreds of flesh indicated that part of the body—the missing hand?—had been devoured here.

It bothered him that he couldn't see any paw prints. The undergrowth was thick, but there were places where the dirt, soon to be mud, showed through.

He needed help to make a second sweep. Where were those guys, anyway? He straightened and looked toward the road, but the rain was falling hard enough to make it difficult to see.

"Sixteen," he said into the Motorola. "Dispatch, this is sixteen."

The storm was interfering with reception, he guessed, because all he heard was static.

His back-up arrived ten minutes later.

"Oh, shit, what a mess."

"Not a pretty sight, is it?"

"Talk about your sloppy eaters. What d'you figure did this? Coyotes?"

"Maybe."

"How long you think it's been lying out here?"

"Do I look like a coroner to you? How the hell should I know?"

"Just asking."

"Don't." He was feeling put out at having to stand in the rain all this while. His socks were wet and made a squishy sound when he walked. "The coroner won't be able to tell the time of death either."

"What makes you think that?"

"You know how they determine how long a person's been dead by sticking that thing that looks like a meat thermometer into the liver?"

"Yeah."

"Well, the liver's gone."

"No fooling?"

"You see it anywhere?"

"Shit, I've seen enough. Cover it up."

He did, and felt better. He felt better still when his back-up, who had six years on him, went and tossed his cookies into the brush.

The rain poured down.

Forty

Katy stood in the living room, holding her mother's overnight case and watching as her Aunt Georgia searched through the hall closet.

"I know I've got a coat you can borrow—"

"Really, don't bother," her mother said. "All I have to do is make it twenty feet to the car. I'm sure it's not raining in LA."

"It's no bother. I don't want you getting wet."

"I'm not the Wicked Witch of the West. I won't melt, will I Katy?"

"Can I plead the Fifth?" Katy asked.

"Katy!"

She gave them her best innocent look. "There was the matter of a pair of ruby slippers."

"I can't believe that my own child is saying these things about the person who controls her allowance and can ground her for life," her mother laughed. "I know I was never that impertinent—"

"Yes, you were." Aunt Georgia handed her a pale blue raincoat. "Here, take this and don't argue."

"Yes ma'am. Well, I guess I'm ready to go." For a moment the two of them stood there, sad-eyed, and then they gave each other a hug.

"Are you sure you want to drive in this rain? The roads must be slick, and going down that mountain could be dangerous."

"I'll be okay. I'm a good driver, believe it or not. Right Katy?"

"She hasn't killed anybody yet."

"Wise guy. Anyway, if I don't get going, I'll run out of daylight before I run out of mountain. I want to get to the interstate before dark."

Katy followed them out to the car. There was a slight overhang from the garage, and they huddled beneath it for a final hug.

"Take care of my little girl—"

"Mom, I'm *eight*," she protested. As far as she was concerned, that was the ultimate argument, but they ignored her.

"—and don't let her con you."

"Don't worry," Aunt Georgia said. "I'm on to her."

That was what Katy needed to hear. She made a face and her mother reached over to muss her hair.

"Listen . . . take care of yourself, too. Do what you have to."

"I will."

"Okay, squirt, give me a kiss."

Katy did as she was asked, holding tight, breathing in the familiar scent of her mother's perfume. "I'll miss you, Mom."

Arms tightened around her. "Look at me, I'm going to cry." She kissed Katy's ear. "I'll miss you too, baby. Be good, you hear?"

Katy closed her eyes; she hadn't thought it would feel like this. She was ready to change her mind, and ask to go on home now. She missed her own bed, and the apartment, and her friends in the building.

Eight years old or not, she'd never spent a night away from her mom before.

The problem was, her mother had taken her aside this morning and explained to her that Aunt Georgia was thinking of getting a divorce. They'd had a long talk and they both thought it would be a good thing if she stayed for Jill's sake.

Aunt Georgia hadn't told Jill yet, and no one knew how she'd take the news. Katy knew from having seen it happen to friends at school that some kids took it hard. It might make it easier for Jill to have her to talk to.

Besides, it probably wasn't going to be a whole five days before she got to go home. A day or two was what her mother had said.

She could stick it out for a day or two.

In spite of her resolve, when her mother released her and turned away, Katy nearly cried out.

Aunt Georgia put her hand on Katy's shoulder, and they stood watching and waving until the car turned the corner and drove out of sight.

Even then Katy stood there, listening as the sound of the engine faded away, and feeling strangely bereft.

"Come on, honey," Aunt Georgia said. "You're shivering. Come inside and I'll make hot chocolate. That'll warm you up."

But it didn't.

Jill had stayed in the bedroom, and she was curled up among three or four pillows when Katy came in.

"Did your mother go?"

Katy nodded and flopped on the bed. "What are you doing?"

"Resting."

"Are you really sick?"

Her cousin's gray-green eyes met hers. "I am."

"Hmm." She drew her legs to her and wrapped her arms around them, then propped her chin on her knees.

253

"You don't look sick."

Jill said nothing.

"Of course, sometimes I pretend to be sick when I'm not so I can stay home from school, but you've got—" she counted on her fingers "—seven days off, not including today. If I were you, I'd save it."

"I'm not pretending."

Katy shrugged. "Okay." She was ready to change the subject.

Jill, apparently, was not. She sat up and hugged a pillow to her. "I may be dying."

"Oh. Camille," Katy said, but with a smile. "That's what my mother calls me when she thinks I'm acting sickly. 'Doing Camille?' she says. But you should see her when she has a cold."

"You should have gone with her."

"What?"

"I like you. You should have gone."

Katy blinked, confused, but when she asked her cousin what she'd meant by that, Jill wouldn't answer.

The storm outside was worsening, and even though it was only three o'clock, the darkness of the clouds made it almost seem like night.

Maybe that was why she was so drowsy. She was lying on her bed, trying to read *Black Beauty* which her aunt had brought home from the library, but her eyes kept wanting to close.

Jill was sound asleep.

The door to the bedroom opened and Aunt Georgia peeked in. "Katy?"

"Yes?" They were both whispering.

"I've got to go out for a little while. I won't be long, maybe an hour or so. If you need anything, I've left the number where I'll be by the phone in the kitchen. Or you can call Faye Paxton; her number's there, too."

"Okay. Aunt Georgia?"

"What is it, honey?"

"Can I ask you a question?"

"Sure."

"Is Jill sick?"

Her aunt frowned. "She is, but the doctor told me it wasn't serious. Why?"

Katy closed her book and sat up, but all at once felt hesitant. How could she ask if Jill was going to die? If it was true, her aunt must feel terrible about it. If it wasn't true, it was not a very nice thing to ask.

"Is something wrong, Katy?"

Katy lowered her eyes; she couldn't do it. "No," she said. "Everything's fine."

Forty-One

The nurse handed Cheryl a clipboard. "Read this. It says, in a nutshell, that you are signing yourself out of the hospital against medical advice. It releases the hospital and your doctor from responsibility if you go home and collapse or something."

"Something?"

"You never know," the nurse said. "If you still want to go through with it, sign here." She pointed to a line on the printed form.

Cheryl scanned the sheet quickly, then accepted the pen the nurse held out to her, and scribbled her name. She gave both back to the nurse. "Thank you."

"I hope you know what you're doing." The nurse signed on the witness line, glanced at her watch, then wrote down the time and date. She stuck the pen in her pocket, then tore the pink copy of the tri-colored form free, and handed it to Cheryl. "There you are; you're free to go. Good luck, Miss Appleton."

"I'm going to need it," Cheryl said.

As he'd promised, Noah Huston was waiting for her in front of the hospital in a sleek-looking sports car.

How in the world was she going to contort her aching, stiff body into that low-slung seat?

Huston got out of the car and came running up the stairs with an open umbrella as she was making her way down, wincing with every jarring step.

"How are you?" he asked, taking her arm.

"I feel like Frankenstein's monster. Put a couple bolts in my neck and I think I've got a career."

"Feeling pretty stiff?"

"You could say that." Her knee and ankle joints seemed to be fused, and her muscles felt tight, stinging from the effort.

"Well, that's to be expected."

"Maybe you expected it, but wait until you have to tie me to the fender of your car to get me home."

He laughed. "We'll get you inside."

"If we do," she said doubtfully, "we may never get me out again."

"Leave it to me. Remember, doctors know a lot about anatomy."

His own was pretty great, Cheryl noted, and then felt her color begin to rise.

"You're over-exerting yourself," he said, "your face is flushed. Lean on me."

Cheryl was more than happy to do as the doctor ordered.

Huston was as good as his word. Somehow he manipulated her bruised and protesting limbs into the car, although they both got rained on in the process. He even fastened her seat belt for her.

Maybe there was something to be said for being incapacitated.

As difficult as it had been, she had to admit that when they drove away from the hospital, she felt better than she had a right to feel.

Except for the cold lump in the pit of her stomach.

"Are you scared?" he asked.

"You read my mind." She rubbed her hands together to warm them. Her fingers were so cold they ached. "I told you I'm a coward."

"I don't believe that." He glanced at her. "You're here."

She took a breath and held it, then released it in a sigh. "I'm here, but I still don't know if what we're doing is the right thing."

"It is."

For a moment, the only sound was that of the windshield wipers. In the distance, lightning flashed, followed by a roll of thunder.

The weather was appropriate, she thought. All that was missing was the eerie music.

"Noah, do you know what'll happen to you if you . . . if you do what you're planning?"

"I do," Huston said and nodded. "I'll turn myself in to the police and they'll arrest me. Eventually, I'll go to jail."

"Will you lose your license to practice medicine?"

"I imagine so." He smiled faintly. "The medical establishment tends to take a dim view of doctors who commit felonies. But it doesn't matter."

"How can you say that? I mean, I don't know you very well, and maybe it's none of my business, but what you're doing—make that what *we're* doing—is going to ruin your life."

"I accept that."

"I don't." She watched his hands as he turned the steering wheel and they even looked like a doctor's hands to her, strong and capable.

A killer's hands?

"Isn't there another way?" she asked, feeling a little

desperate now that the time was near.

"We've been over this before."

In fact, they'd discussed it at length, long past the time when visiting hours were over. "Doctor's privilege," he'd said then.

He was willing, it seemed, to give all of that up. Privilege, prestige, the respect afforded to professionals who'd sacrificed years of their lives in the service to others.

He might wind up sacrificing his life as well; California had reinstated the death penalty in 1972 and although no one had yet been executed, the gas chamber was ready and waiting.

"We could go to the police," she said, "and tell them everything we know."

"They wouldn't believe us."

"You don't know that." They were nearing the street where she lived, and suddenly it seemed urgent that she convince him they were making a mistake. "You told me you've kept a record of all the things you've found out, names and dates of the kids who she's hurt—"

"Who *I* say she's hurt. I can't prove it."

"What about Sarah Lassiter? She told you she thinks Jill is a witch. And Kevin, you could talk to him. I'm sure there are other kids—"

"Do you think if I marched into the sheriff's office with a gang of kids and told them a story about witches and goblins they'd believe me?"

"But—"

"Even if they did, even if the sheriff believes in the bogeyman and we managed to convince them, what do you think they'd do?"

Cheryl was silent.

"Nothing," he answered for her. "She's seven years old. I can't see anyone filing a complaint charging her with assault—"

"I'd do it."

"Then the school board and your principal really would insist on having your head examined."

She knew he was right.

"The point I'm making," he cautioned, "is that asking the law to handle it won't work. The legal system doesn't recognize that a power like Jill's could exist. If they did anything at all, they'd investigate. We haven't time to wait for the wheels of justice to turn."

They pulled into her drive and he killed the engine. With the wipers off, the windshield was sheeted by rain.

Cheryl frowned. "It's a high price you're paying," she said quietly.

"Look, if you'd rather not go through with this, tell me. I'll understand."

"It isn't that." She blinked. "Well, actually, it is that, but it doesn't seem as though either one of us has a choice."

"All you have to do is make the call and leave the rest to me."

It sounded so simple. Why did she have the feeling it was not?

The nurse had helped her get dressed at the hospital and she hadn't realized how difficult it would be to change her clothes. By the time she'd struggled into a pair of jeans and a black turtleneck sweater, she was damp with perspiration and short of breath.

Even a simple thing like tying her shoelaces became a major project. She knotted both laces so they wouldn't come undone at an inopportune moment.

"Like when I'm running for my life," she said, gingerly getting to her feet. "At zero miles per hour."

She found Noah in her dining room, sitting at the table with an array of medical supplies before him. He was

261

holding a small bottle with a gray rubber seal and as she watched he plunged a needle through the seal.

He held the bottle upside down and retracted the plunger on the syringe.

The barrel of the syringe slowly began to fill with a clear liquid.

Cheryl bit her lip. "Is that it?"

"Yes." Noah hadn't taken his eyes from the bottle.

"Will it work?"

"It should."

"If it doesn't?"

"Then we punt."

And run like hell, she thought, which means I'm going to be shit out of luck.

"I have something for you, too," he said. He withdrew the needle, capped it with a little blue plastic sheath, and put it on the table.

"You mean like those drugs they give race horses so they can run faster? Or at all?"

"No." He tore two squares off a narrow sheet of individually bubble-packed tablets.

"What is it?"

"Valium."

"Why are you giving me these?" she asked as he put them in her hand.

"So you won't be nervous."

"You'd better give me more."

And then the time had come for her to make the call. Noah dialed the number she'd found in her records and handed her the phone.

Forty-Two

Jill had been listening for the phone, and when it rang she unfolded her legs from beneath her and crawled off the bed.

"I'll get that if you want," Katy offered, looking up from her book.

"No. It's for me."

The storm seemed to have stalled overhead, blocking whatever daylight was left, and the hall was dim, but six years in this house had prepared her to walk through it in darkness.

She preferred it.

Jill reached the kitchen as the phone rang for the fifth time. She waited until it had rung twice more, and then lifted the receiver.

"Hello, Miss Appleton," she said. "I thought you'd be calling."

"Jill?"

"Yes."

"How did you—"

"Know it was you? I know a lot of things, Miss Appleton."

There was silence at the other end.

Jill smiled.

263

"Is your mother home?" her teacher asked after a minute had passed.

"My mother? Why would you want to talk to my mother? I'm not in any trouble at school, am I?" she said, and laughed softly.

"No, no trouble. I just wondered—"

"If I'm alone?"

"Are you?"

"You know, I really don't think I should answer you," Jill said. "Maybe you're not Miss Appleton at all. Maybe I made a mistake just now, and you only *sound* like Miss Appleton."

"Jill . . ."

"Maybe you're one of those sick people they're always warning little kids about. 'Don't ever tell anyone who calls that you're home alone,'" she mimicked. "Are you sick, Miss Appleton?"

"You know it's me."

"Maybe you're planning to come to my house and break in. Maybe you want to kill me."

Jill heard the gasp from her teacher and was pleased. "Is that it? Am I right? Do you want to kill me, Miss Appleton?"

"I don't know why you're saying these things, but I wish you'd stop."

"I can't stop."

"Yes, you can."

Jill heard a difference in her tone and realized that Miss Appleton was using her teacher's voice. She wondered why; it had had little effect on the kids in school. What made her think it would work now?

"I have to go, Miss Appleton."

"Jill—"

"I have a lot to do."

"No, wait—"

Jill smiled again at the panic she heard. "I'll be expecting you," she said.

She hung up.

After a moment of reflection, she extended a finger and touched the phone. Within seconds, thick black smoke began to pour out around the edges where it rested against the wall.

She really didn't want to be disturbed by any more calls.

"What's going on?"

Jill turned to see Katy standing in the doorway. Her cousin, barefooted, had come into the kitchen without her having heard. Or perhaps her own preoccupation had been a factor.

Either way, it was an unacceptable lapse. She would have to make sure it didn't happen again.

"Something the matter with the phone?"

Jill glanced at it. The smoke had cleared, but the plastic casing had warped from the heat, and the wall was sooty behind it.

"We had a little fire," she said.

"Is it out?"

"For now."

Katy gave her a wide-eyed look. "What's wrong with you? You sound strange."

Jill only returned her gaze.

"I think you'd better lie down again," Katy said, and then her eyes darted back to the phone. "I was thinking, I should call your mom."

"No. You should leave."

"*What?*"

"If you leave now, you won't be hurt."

"Jill," Katy said, her hands on her hips, "you're acting

265

very weird."

"I have no desire to see you injured," she said, and was vaguely surprised to find that she meant it.

"What are you talking about?"

"Get out, Katy Wright, while you can."

For the first time, there was a hint of uncertainty in the other girl's eyes. Jill could feel the pressures inside begin to mount, and she knew that before too many more minutes passed she would no longer be able to control her own impulses.

"Please," Jill said. It wasn't a word she often used.

"But . . . it's raining."

Jill held out her right hand, the palm up. "Watch," she commanded.

She took a quick breath and exhaled a thin stream of black. At first the Source resembled nothing more than a puff of smoke, except that it remained hovering above her hand. But gradually, by force of will, she transformed it into a shape.

A tree.

It had three dimensions, but no substance, and it was possible to see through it. The detail was impressive, down to the scarring of the trunk and leaves which seemed to move in response to the wind.

The tree was a holographic representation of a tree across the road.

Jill raised her hand, bringing it closer to her face, and studied what she'd created.

"How did you do that?" Katy breathed.

"It doesn't matter. Do you see?"

Katy nodded.

"Go to the window and look out."

Katy nearly skidded across the floor as she ran to the window. "Oh!"

"Yes?"

266

When she turned, her face showed her amazement. "It's the same tree."

"Watch that one," Jill ordered.

With obvious reluctance, Katy looked out the window again.

Jill brought her left hand up, circled it over the shape and then touched the image with her index finger. The tree burst into flames.

Even from where she was standing, she could see the glow as the real tree did the same.

"Shit!" Katy said, and then covered her mouth with both hands.

"I want you to go now."

"That wasn't a trick, was it?" Katy's eyes were bright. "You did it for real."

She inclined her head.

"And the other stuff? It isn't a magic box."

"No."

"What else can you do?"

Jill had no time to listen to any more of this. "Do what you wish."

They were coming, and she had to be done before they got here.

She left the kitchen for the front room. She sat down on the floor, closed her eyes, and released all of the Source from her lungs.

For seven years, she had been the Keeper of the Source, but now her lifetask was done. There was some satisfaction in that . . .

Carefully, she began to shape the Source into a replica of the town of Winslow.

It took more effort that she had anticipated, and her body was shivering by the time she was done. There was a pain in her abdomen, a twisting, pulling pain that made her gasp.

She brushed a hand across her forehead which was damp with sweat.

Time was up, and there was nothing—no one—to stop her.

Forty-Three

Abner Cosgrove was beginning to regret whatever rash and foolish impulse had led him to agree to see Georgia Baker this afternoon. It was a sweep of the minute hand away from five o'clock and the woman had been talking without pause for almost an hour now.

He'd been taking notes all along, nodding when she looked to him for a response, and grunting when it seemed to be called for.

The tea his housekeeper had made for them no doubt was tepid in the pot and totally undrinkable.

Once or twice he had tried to suggest that perhaps she was ahead of herself, worrying about things like division of property at what was really only the first inning of the game.

Nothing he'd said appeared to get through to her, and he'd given up for the time being.

It was a common reaction to filing for divorce, this verbal diarrhea. Women in particular suffered from it, probably, he supposed, because in most bad marriages communication was one of the first things to go, and they'd had no one to listen to them for a while.

Cosgrove was sympathetic, but sympathy only went so far.

His dinner would be served promptly at five-thirty, and he intended to have a hot, proper meal. His roast beef and steamed vegetables would not go the way of the tea.

To that end, he cleared his throat loudly, and with some authority.

She'd been pacing throughout her diatribe, but she stopped and looked at him as if she'd forgotten he was in the room.

"Mrs. Baker," he said, "I can see that you're upset, but I think I've got enough here to have my secretary start on the paperwork first thing in the morning."

"Yes, if you would."

"If I might just go over the high points," he said, and referred to his notes. "Baker versus Baker. You wish a divorce on the grounds of irreconcilable differences in a marriage of some thirteen years. There is one child, a girl, who was legally adopted by you and your soon-to-be former husband approximately six years ago. You are requesting that custody of the child be awarded to you, and agree to reasonable visitation rights."

"Including two weeks in the summer if he wants. I don't think he will."

"We'll see. You also agree to forego spousal support, but request child support in the amount of two hundred and fifty dollars a month. You request that Mr. Baker continue to provide adequate health insurance for the child, and that he contribute equally to her education should she wish to go to college."

"Yes, and the property—"

"I think we'll need to talk about the property further; it's a good deal more complex than the rest of this."

"I know, but—"

"Let me finish with the routine matters." At her nod, he continued: "Regarding the joint indebtedness, you propose that all open accounts, exclusive of those for real estate, be paid on an equal basis. You will retain

270

possession and ownership of one of the two family vehicles; he will keep the other. Each party will be responsible for the payments for their vehicle."

"That's fair, isn't it?" she asked a bit anxiously. "I mean, there's more money owing on his Blazer, but it's worth more, too."

"Yes, Mrs. Baker, it's quite fair." He took off his reading glasses and frowned at her. "Why don't you sit down? You look a little pale."

"I'm fine. About the property?"

Cosgrove sighed. Persistence, thy name is woman. "Very well. You are proposing that you be allowed to have sole claim to your pending inheritance from your late father, for which concession you are willing to relinquish any claim to certain community property assets, including equity in your house and co-ownership in the business, and profit from the sale of the same."

"Right."

"Before I'll let you agree to these last matters, I think we'll need to have appraisals done on both properties. You may be giving away the farm, Mrs. Baker."

"I need the cash now. You told me that my father's estate could be settled within a week."

"That's very true." He refrained from mentioning that had she not been so stubborn, the estate could have been settled months ago.

Sometimes his restraint amazed him.

"I want to be free to make a new life for my daughter and myself."

That was also a common theme in divorce. "New lives aren't always for the better," he said. "Take my word for it, Mrs. Baker, I know."

"Our lives will be."

"Hmm." He placed his pencil on the pad and leaned back in his chair, steepling his hands and regarding her over his fingertips. For a woman on the verge of a better

271

life, she looked almost ill.

"Well," she said, "I've taken up enough of your time."

"Indeed. My secretary will call you to let you know when to come in and sign the papers."

"Thank you, Mr. Cosgrove. For everything."

"There'll be time enough for that after I've done something," he said, "like keep you from making a foolish mistake."

She smiled and started towards him, her hand outstretched as if to shake his when, without warning, all the color left her face, and she pitched forward.

Cosgrove wasn't spry enough to catch her, but he rounded the desk and knelt by her side where she lay on the floor. He placed his hand against her throat and felt a strong pulse.

Thank God for that.

He got up and went to the door, called down the hall for his housekeeper, then returned to her side, cradling her head in his lap.

"Mercy me, Mr. Cosgrove," the housekeeper said. "What's happened to the poor woman?"

"I'll be damned if I know. Get me a cold cloth and I'll see if I can bring her around."

"Yes sir," the housekeeper said, and bustled off.

But a few seconds later her eyelashes fluttered open and she looked at him.

"It's Jill," she whispered.

He hadn't a notion as to what she was talking about and was about to ask when the room started to shake.

"My God, Jill."

Forty-Four

The destruction began at Meadowbrook Elementary,
where Roland Barry had gone, as he did every Sunday,
for the express purpose of avoiding his in-laws.

It had been a mistake to agree to live within a thousand
miles of the wife's family, a mistake he'd paid for dearly
with the invasion of his home each and every Sunday by
"the folks."

His father-in-law wasn't a bad sort, but the old woman
had never heard a comment she wouldn't argue to the
death. Her tongue was razor fine, honed from decades of
use, and she wielded it with the skill of a master
swordsman, most often against him.

Triple-chinned but fierce, the snap of that woman's
jaws would put the fear of God into any man.

So he excused himself by pleading unfinished work
and came down to the school where he largely did
nothing more than wander the empty halls passing time.

The old woman had long since bitten off, chewed, and
spit out whatever backbone her own husband had once
had, and she never would dream of fussing at her "little
girl," that precious bundle of joy who was now flirting
with the two hundred pound indicator on the bathroom
scale.

If he wasn't home, the old woman got bored at having no one to bitch at, and finally would leave.

Then he could go home.

For now, he amused himself in the kindergarten room spelling out a few choice words with the alphabet blocks.

The floor beneath him began to shake.

Earthquake, he thought, and imagined the squeals of the children if school were in session.

The floor kept shaking, so he mixed the blocks up—it wouldn't do for the kiddies to come back to school after vacation and find a message from the principal—and turned to walk calmly to the doorway.

By the time he'd taken four steps, he was ready to take a dive toward the door.

The beautiful wooden floor was breaking up, planks cracking and splintering like dry kindling. The concrete beneath had crumbled and sent up a cloud of choking dust, and the ground bucked and heaved.

Mr. Barry saw at once that the doorway wasn't going to be protection enough; the entire building was at risk. Of all the fates he'd seen for himself, being trapped under a ton of rubble was not one he'd care to meet.

He landed hard on his knees, and his left shin was pierced by a huge splinter. He rolled over onto his back—the floor rolling beneath him—and bent his knee, bringing his leg up within reach.

There wasn't time for proper first-aid measures and he just grabbed the jagged chunk of wood and yanked it out of his flesh.

He was bleeding.

It sickened him, but he knew this was not the time or place to worry about it. If he got out, he could wrap a handkerchief or something around his calf to stem the flow of blood. If he *didn't* get out of here, he was likely to die beneath a collapsed ceiling joist.

But don't think of that, he told himself sternly,

fighting his way onto his hands and knees and beginning to crawl into the hallway.

All around him, ceiling tiles were falling and dust was swirling. The overhead light fixtures were breaking free of their braces and the long fluorescent bulbs were popping and disintegrating into a shower of glass.

He kept his head down and concentrated on the front doors which were now only about ten feet away.

Opposite him, the door to the girls' bathroom was flung open by some unseen force, and he saw that the pipes had burst, with water spraying everywhere. His principal's eye noted that the paper towel dispenser beside the sinks was empty.

No wonder the children had so many colds in this school; the kids didn't wash their hands because they couldn't dry them.

The mirror above the sinks had cracked and now a huge triangular section of it fell away. It hit the edge of the sink and broke into wickedly sharp fragments.

"Seven years of bad luck," he mumbled.

The doors were now almost within reach of his hand and now he recalled that he'd locked them from the inside, and would have to find the key.

As he dug into his pocket with a shaking hand, he envisioned rescuers finding his crushed and mangled body huddled at the door.

Finally he found the keys and inserted the correct key in the lock at approximately the same moment he realized that he smelled smoke.

Barry glanced over his shoulder, saw the flames, and in his haste to pull the door open, hit himself in the head. Hard. He actually heard the sound of his skin splitting open.

Blood splashed into his eyes.

But after coming so far, he would not be denied. He forced the door open against the rubble and squeezed his body through.

Immediately he was soaked through to the skin by a pounding, icy rain, and the shock was such that he nearly turned to go back inside.

An ominous groan from within the building removed that temptation, and he turned, wiped the blood and rain from his face, and looked out across his domain. For a second his eyes refused to believe what he was.

The landscape around the school might have been a special effect from one of those end-of-the-world movies. Not a house in view had been left unscathed. Most were burning, even in this downpour, but some had been reduced by the shaking to a mound of wood, stucco, shingles, and broken glass.

There were people running everywhere. A woman dressed only in a black teddy stood in the middle of what had been the street, waving her arms up and down as if trying to lift off and fly.

Down at the corner, two or more cars had collided, and one of them was billowing black smoke from under its badly crumpled hood. Even at a distance, he could see that there was someone still in the car, and several men were trying to wrench the door open.

They were crazy, he thought. Any idiot could see that the car was going to blow.

The principal staggered down the steps and crossed the circular drive to the lawn. As he reached it, he felt a *whoosh* of air behind him and it picked him up and flung him to the ground.

His face skidded across the wet grass. His lower lip peeled back and his teeth collected the weeds.

Lying splayed out on the lawn, his body was pelted by bits of Meadowbrook Elementary along with the rain.

He closed his eyes just as the bell began to ring.

*   *   *

When it seemed that the worst of it was over, Barry sat up, picked some of the turf out of his teeth, and looked at what remained of his school.

It was much worse than he'd imagined.

There wasn't even a mound. The building had been flattened as if a giant steamroller had driven it into the ground. There was not a single identifiable *anything* that he could see.

Not a desk, not a blackboard, not a metal locker or wooden cubbyhole . . . not a blasted thing.

Totalled.

Behind him, there was an odd sound, strangely familiar and yet he couldn't place it. A creak, a clang, somehow metallic, and yet?

Barry turned to look a split second before the flagpole—the last thing standing—collapsed and struck him dead.

Forty-Five

Huston had been forced by the upheaval to abandon
the car, with Cheryl Appleton still in it—and set out on
foot for the Baker house.

He ran through the rain with his head down, dodging
the worst of the holes in the road, and staying well clear
of the structures which might give way. The people he
saw looked dazed and bloodied, and none seemed aware of
him as he ran by.

Overhead, the thick dark clouds were almost low
enough to touch, and they churned continuously, lit
here and there by lightning, and still spilling rain.

His breath vaporized and joined the clouds.

Almost there.

Huston rounded a corner and came upon a huge crater
in the road. The bottom was filled with water and sewage
from busted pipes, and there was, he saw, someone
floating face down in the muck.

"Damn it, Jill," he swore.

He skirted the edge of the crater and continued on.
There was a stitch in his side from running, and a careless
step had left him with a turned knee, but he forced
himself to keep going.

He had to stop her before she finished, or they'd all

be lost.

Finally he reached the street, which was oddly quiet
and displayed none of the destruction he'd seen
elsewhere, except for an old oak tree that had burned to a
black hulk.

As he neared the Baker house, he saw a little girl
huddling under the overhang in front of the garage. She
wore overalls and a white t-shirt, but her feet were bare
and she looked miserable and cold.

Her hair was plastered to her head, and she pushed it
out of her face, rising to her feet as he approached.

"It's not magic," she said, and sniffed.

Huston took off his jacket and put it around her.
"What's going on inside?"

"I don't know."

He sat on his heels so that he could look in her face.
"How can I get in the house?"

"I don't know," she repeated through chattering
teeth.

"Come on, now. You have to help me. Where is Jill?"

For a moment he thought she might not answer, but
she drew a breath and said, "In the living room."

"Okay, good. How did you get out here? The front
door?"

"No. The kitchen. There's a porch."

"Is the door unlocked? Can I get in?"

She gave him an incredulous look. "Why do you want
to go in there?"

"I want to stop her."

The girl laughed. "You can't."

"Maybe not, but I have to try." He straightened and
glanced across the street at his own house, which was
dark but appeared intact. "You can't stay here in the
rain. Take my keys and go to the house," he said

and pointed.

"What are you going to do?"

He didn't answer. Given what he'd seen on the way, he wondered if he could do anything, or if she would destroy him as she had the town.

"Go now," he said, and gave her a gentle push in that direction.

The girl took a half-dozen steps and then stopped, turning to face him. "This is real, isn't it?"

"I'm afraid so."

When she turned again he started around the corner of the garage toward the backyard.

He needn't have worried about having to break into the house; the back door was standing open. He hurried to it and stepped inside, closing it after him.

In contrast to the sounds of wind and rain, it was almost unnaturally quiet in the house. Even the drops of water from his clothes made no noise as they fell to the kitchen floor.

The air felt thick and had an acrid smell. It burned his eyes.

He noticed the wallphone was unusable but since he doubted any of the phone lines in town were working, it made little difference.

Who would he call, anyway?

Huston walked as quietly as he could to the kitchen door and pushed it open. He stood and listened.

Whatever she was doing, it wasn't making any noise.

He withdrew the capped syringe from his pants pocket, positioned it in his hand so that it wouldn't be visible, and slipped through the door.

When he turned into the hall, his eyes were drawn to the living room. At this angle, he could only see a corner of it, but he felt a jolt of surprise. He hadn't know what to expect, but certainly not this.

The town of Winslow was laid out before him, and like

the real one, it was in ruins.

He took a step closer, and closer, until he stood in the doorway and could see it all.

With the exception of a few houses on the very outskirts of town and a few in this neighborhood, nothing had been left standing. He didn't know the layout well enough to identify some of the buildings, but clearly the hospital was gone, as was the octagonal Senior Center he'd passed when driving Cheryl to her home.

Even the crater in the road was represented, down to the bubbling effluent.

The only details not in the model were the people.

"How do you like it?" a voice asked.

Huston saw her then, sitting Indian-style on the floor at the edge of her creation.

She was smiling.

Wisps of smoke flowed over her naked body, and he saw that there was a black cord, a monstrous umbilical cord, which attached at her navel.

It writhed and pulsed with a life of its own, but he did not see the terminus.

"Have you come to cut me free again?" she said, and her voice echoed inside his brain.

"What are you?"

She did not answer, but made a motion with her hand, and one of the standing houses began to crumble.

As it did, he heard the screams of terror, a child's voice cut off mid-cry, and he stared at Jill, watching the play of some emotion—satisfaction? elation?—across her pale face.

"Where's Miss Appleton?" she asked when that building was demolished. "Did she stay at home? Too bad. I doubt she could get out in time, do you think?"

"No."

"Ah well, she hadn't many students left, anyway. A few survived, but they won't be going to school for a long time, I suppose."

His mind struggled to make sense of this. "Stop it," he said, and knew he sounded foolish. "You've done enough."

The child seemed to consider that, her gray-green eyes surveying what she'd done. The tip of her tongue moistened her lips and then she smiled.

"Very well. If it pleases you."

"It would please me if you'd undo this." He gestured at the ravaged miniature town.

Her expression was amused. "Even you must know that I can't do that."

His hand tightened around the syringe.

"Don't bother," she said.

Against his will, his hand was forced open and the syringe dropped to the floor.

"You doctors have delusions of power, you think you hold the key to life and death, but nothing that you have in your medical arsenal can touch me."

She opened her eyes fractionally wider, and it felt as if a hand were on his chest, pushing him back into the wall.

"Get away," she said, dismissively. "Before I decide to let you have a taste of what you intended for me. Would you like that?"

The pressure on his chest increased and he shook his head.

"I thought not. It doesn't seem a pleasant way to die. Unable to move, unable to breathe, but still alert enough to know what's happening to you. A horrible thing to do to a child, Dr. Huston."

"You're not a child," he whispered.

"Am I not? You delivered me, didn't you?"

"I don't know what the hell you are."

"No?"

"Or why you needed me to—"

"Bring me forth? We can't cross over without a

human hand. That's why you're here now, and why I let you live. You have to deliver me once again, Doctor, to my next form. This—" she indicated her body "—is the larval stage."

"God—"

"Has nothing to do with it. It's almost time, I think. You will do it, won't you?"

"If I say no?"

She merely smiled. "Come now." She extended her hand to him.

He had no choice but to take it.

Around him, the Baker house faded away.

Huston was in a place he knew somehow was distant and yet familiar.

It was very dark, and he had to hold onto its hand, which no longer felt like a hand, but something soft and boneless.

There was absolutely no sound, and the silence seemed to press against his ear drums.

Gradually he realized that it was no longer cold, and indeed was becoming uncomfortably warm and humid.

The child led him to a low platform on which were the rudimentary tools of delivery. There she let go of his hand, and in the dim light he could see that there was movement of some kind under her skin which had thinned to the point of being transparent.

At first he stood there, uncertain of what was expected of him, but after a moment, his instincts took over.

There were two lengths of a glossy black material which he used to tie off the umbilical cord. It took every ounce of strength he had to pull them tight, but he was afraid of what might flow from the cord when he cut it if the ligatures weren't taut.

The child's eyes were watching him.

284

His fingers closed around a silver knife. *Do I plunge it into her heart?*

He thought of the devastation she'd caused, the lost lives, the human misery, and the pain, and his hand clenched as he raised it, holding it like a dagger.

Why wasn't she stopping him?

Why did she just lie there?

Now, he thought, *now*.

It was as if he were being sucked through a wind tunnel, a great roaring and the feel of air bracing his skin. All was dark, and motion, and it went on and on.

His lungs ached to take a breath, but he could not, and then the darkness was within him and he knew nothing more for a time.

He came to on the floor of the Baker living room.

"Are you alive?" a voice asked.

Huston lifted his head off the floor. A few feet away, sitting on the couch, was the other little girl.

The real one.

"I think so," he said.

"Where's Jill?"

He swallowed; his throat ached. "She's gone."

"Did you kill her?"

"No," he whispered. "No."

Epilogue

Katy loved Los Angeles.

It felt wonderful to be home. Her Aunt Georgia had taken over her bedroom, and she had to sleep on the couch, but she would have gladly slept on the floor if it meant being home.

And away from Winslow, or what remained of it.

They'd spent five days in Leland, which was nearby, so that they could attend Jill's funeral. She guessed the reason it took so long was because there were so many funerals going on.

But it was the first funeral Katy'd been to—her mother hadn't wanted to go to her grandfather's—and even though she'd seen lots of them in the movies, she hadn't known what it would be like in real life. It turned out not to be too bad.

Everyone wore black or dark colors, and Aunt Georgia had even worn a veil.

The casket was small, and white. There wasn't a "viewing," whatever that was.

The organ music was nice, kind of somber, but it helped cover the sounds of people crying.

There had been all kinds of flowers in the church, and the fragrance of them was nearly overwhelming. Katy had been relieved when that part was over and they could go outside for a breath of fresh air.

They gathered around the gravesite, and the minister read from the Bible.

Some of the words were familiar to her.

Some, the wind carried away.

Her mother had sat by Aunt Georgia, holding her aunt's hand between both of hers. Dave sat on the other side, but he didn't take Aunt Georgia's other hand.

After the ceremony, Katy had walked behind them, and though she hadn't tried to listen, she overheard what they said.

"Georgia, I don't know what people have been telling you, but there's nothing between me and Tanya."

"It doesn't matter," her aunt had said in a voice made husky by tears. "There hasn't been anything between us either."

Dave hadn't gotten into the limousine with them when they left. When Katy had looked out the rear window, she saw him still standing there.

It was sad.

But now there was the three of them, and she was home in LA, and everything was going to be all right.

Except for one thing, which kind of still bothered her. She didn't know who to tell, or if she should.

The night before, when she and Jill had been playing, Jill had said something that just stuck with her. At the time it hadn't meant anything, but now . . .

"I'm not the only one," Jill had said. "There are others."